IF THE EARTH FALLS IN

IF THE EARTH FALLS IN

Mavis Thorpe Clark

A Clarion Book

THE SEABURY PRESS · New York

The Seabury Press, 815 Second Avenue, New York, N.Y. 10017

First American Edition 1975

Copyright © 1973 by Mavis Thorpe Clark

This book was first published in Australia under the title
New Golden Mountain.

Printed in the United States of America.

LIBRARY OF CONGRESS CATALOGING IN PUBLICATION DATA

Clark, Mavis Thorpe.
    If the earth falls in.

    "A Clarion book."
    SUMMARY: Resentful of her poverty, a fifteen-year-old
girl decides to run away, but her involvement with two rival
boys leads not to a new life but a fight for survival as all three
are trapped in a caved-in mine shaft.
    [1. Survival—Fiction.   2. Australia—Fiction]
I. Title.
PZ7.C5495If4   [Fic]   75-4781
ISBN 0-8164-3153-1

IF THE EARTH FALLS IN

CHAPTER ONE

The argument between Louise and her aunt had started when Aunt Eva had brought home the dresses the previous evening. There had been sharp words then, followed by a lull until now.

'Lou, you'll break those dishes the way you're handling them!' Aunt Eva's voice, from the room adjoining the kitchen, was flat and grouchy, revealing that she was disturbed.

And so she should be, thought the girl, for taking for granted that she, Louise, would be happy to wear someone else's dress. Well, Eva would be even more disturbed when she found out that—because of the dress—Louise was going to leave her and go to the city. Though the time for this announcement was not yet.

The kitchen was the biggest room in the old stone cottage but still not large, with only one window of four small panes set in the recess between the side wall and the fuel-stove. Yet it was not a dark room, for Eva had recently painted the walls white, and the sun was shining through the glass like indirect lighting. It high-lighted the blobs of white paint that Eva had dropped on the worn, faded lino.

It was a late spring day after days of greyness, and Louise's mood should have lifted to it. But as she dried the last of the lunch dishes only her voice was raised as she answered her aunt.

'I'm not going to wear the dress! I won't!'

Louise was fifteen, thin and leggy but probably as tall as she would grow. Her pale shining hair was parted in the middle

1

and hung dead straight past her shoulders. On week days, complying with High School regulations, she plaited it over her ears and pulled the plaits down tight so that short ends hung around her face. She was proud of its shine, regarding it as one of her few good points, and in school smoothed it often with her hand, comforted by the satin feel.

'You'll do as you're told,' Eva said, and both were glad that she was in the living-room, and they were not confronting each other.

The red dress had pitched the crisis.

There had never been a major clash between them before. Their relationship had been on a curiously level plane—a level of dullness, Louise now felt. But now her silent criticisms of her aunt—of which she had been aware without feeling real rebellion—were suddenly aflame, red as the dress, as though a north wind had whipped up live ashes.

'Mrs Burton was good to give you the dress—the three dresses,' Eva said.

'Pigs to her!'

'She's the mother of your best friend.'

'But you work for her, don't you? You clean her house. Anyway, I haven't seen Sheila for more than six months. How do I know if she's my friend any more?'

'She writes to you.'

'She'll laugh when she knows her mother has given me her old dresses.'

Eva didn't say that Julia Burton, wife of the bank manager, had said to her, 'Your Louise is so quick and imaginative, full of ideas—she'll make something of her life—I'd like to help her.' And Eva had supposed the dresses to be such help.

She had carried them home triumphantly yesterday, after work, and Louise's instant fury had shocked as well as singed. It was so unexpected. Why should Lou worry about wearing the dresses? Kids wore anything these days—even faded their jeans so that they would look scruffy. And the girls were wearing their dresses any length. From just covering the bottom to mid-calf. So why should Lou be upset about wearing Sheila's dresses?

2

'They're good dresses—Mrs Burton always buys the best for Sheila. The two summer ones will be a godsend in the hot weather, and the red wool one is just right for now.'

'They're out-of-date. Too short. That's why she's giving them away. Why doesn't she give them to a Home, or some-where?''

'She knows we can't afford much. It's good of her. You'll put on the wool one when you go to tea there this evening.'

'It's not *my* dress—and I'm *not* going to wear it!' So many people had admired Sheila in that red dress.

It was a cold Saturday afternoon, despite the sun, and from the living-room came the sound of Eva putting another log on the fire and the sparks exploding as she poked the coals with the poker that was worn unevenly at the end. The poker and the tongs and the iron fender had stood on the hearth since grandfather Ed's day, just as his tobacco-cutter, shaped like a miniature axe and chopping-block, still stood on the mantel-piece.

Louise hadn't known her grandfather—Ed Turnbull—or great-grandfather William Turnbull, who had started a family on the goldfields. But she knew them both through Eva's eyes, and sometimes she hated them both. She hated them because they had lived on in this mining town, lived on in this cottage overlooking the gully from which so much gold had been won, when there was a world beyond. Great-grandfather William had worked the alluvial in the creeks but he had never struck it rich, and when the gold was very elusive he had made a living by doing fencing, odd jobs or seasonal work. He had died leaving this cottage, built on a plot of ground which was held on a Miner's Right, and a family.

His widow had had to work hard to rear her young children, and became washerwoman and ironer for the townspeople. Her earnings hadn't stretched to education to make them more than labourers; while a treat for them, when they came hungry from school, was a 'piece', cut thick from the loaf she had baked herself, spread thick with dripping and with each child's initials outlined in brown sugar or treacle.

Grandfather Ed had worked underground, burrowing in the

deep quartz mines owned by big companies, and had continued to live on in the cottage until he died of fracture smoke and rock dust. Even so he reached seventy-two which spoke well, other miners said, for the staying power of Ed Turnbull.

Louise's knowledge of her male line stopped at grandfather. She knew almost nothing of her father. Eva didn't talk about him. He had come casually in from the city, married her mother, Rosemary, and gone again, abandoning her and her baby. Rosemary had died shortly afterwards; and that had left only Eva, who was three years older than Rosemary, and Louise.

Eva seemed to think it was a good thing her father hadn't stayed around. She considered him a no-good who didn't like work, and who had dazzled her young sister with his city ways. He was not real to Louise because grandfather Ed and great-grandfather William were the ones Eva always talked about. Louise didn't think of her father very much.

She finished drying the last cup and hung it on a hook of the open dresser.

With the towel placed to dry near the stove, Louise moved to the side of the doorway leading into the living-room and picked up the soft, loosely tied newspaper parcel she had hidden under the chair cushion. Then she hurried across the narrow verandah, wired-in against flies and mosquitoes, and which, like all old mining cottages, had a steeply sloped iron skillion roof.

She went quickly. The parcel had to be hidden again, outside the house. She didn't stop even to speak to the cat, Millie, who was curled in a weathered cane chair in the corner. She had found the starving, deserted kitten, barely old enough to have her eyes open, in a patch of blackberry on the creek bank. She had scratched her hands and knees in its rescue and for weeks had fed the kitten from a doll's feeding bottle. Then, strangely enough, Eva had taken over the cat, buying sheeps' hearts for her from the butcher, letting her in to sit by the fire or the stove, and often fondling her. The last was the most surprising, for Eva was slow to show affection to anyone. Not like Mrs Burton who had always kissed Sheila good-night—every night—until she'd gone to boarding-school.

Now Millie was sleek and heavy with her third litter of

4

kittens; and Louise was glad that Eva would have the cat and the kittens to occupy her after she'd gone. For, last night, she had made up her mind to go. To leave Eva. The red dress had decided her.

As she hastened along the path crowded with woody fuchsias and a snaking grapevine, flagged with slabs of slate from the mine-heads, towards the apple tree in the bottom corner of the yard, her mind was still with that decision. To get away she had to raise money, and to do so she was going to use the Chinese painting on glass—*steal* was too strong a word, she felt—which Eva kept on top of her wardrobe in her bedroom.

It was only this morning that she had thought of using the Chinese painting. She had had to take a message to Mrs Burton—that was when Julia Burton had invited her back to tea—and she had passed a Chinese man just before she reached the bank.

Her imagination had immediately replaced his well-cut overcoat, leather gloves, and peaked tweed cap with a picture of a Chinese digger in dark blue cotton trousers and jacket, slippers of worked silk with wooden soles that turned up at the toes, coolie hat, and a long black pig-tail. These Chinese gold-seekers had called Australia *Hsin-chin-shan*—'New Golden Mountain'.

Louise was well-informed about the Chinese on the goldfields. Firstly, because history to her was not just a school subject but a tapestry of story and picture, and secondly because Sheila's father. had made it his policy to become an authority on local history. And Dan Burton liked to talk.

This Chinese looked like a successful business man, and he walked with quiet confidence along the street, busy with Saturday morning shoppers in from farm or orchard.

It was a long time since a Chinese man had walked along this street with its old-fashioned shopfronts and verandah posts. Yet over a century ago, when the town had been the hub for the greatest alluvial goldfields the world had ever known, a quarter of the gold-diggers had been Chinese, most of them re-working the 'tailings' left by the Europeans. True they had been a segregated population, living in their own Chinatown,

5

having their own shops and Joss House. The last of these olive-skinned men had disappeared from the country-side several decades ago.

This morning the Chinese man had passed quickly from sight, but he had caused Louise to remember the painting done on glass. Not that it didn't figure often in the stories she made up when lying under the cool of the apple tree in summer heat with busy bush flies whirring, or in those moments of soft warmth before going to sleep on a winter's night. The painting was a story in itself. Now it would figure in a real life story. Fleetingly, she hoped that Chan Ah-Foo would not be displeased.

Louise stopped at the apple tree. The sun was polishing the new green leaves that hid the knotted frame. The tree leaned badly, struggling out to the light from between the fence and the wreck of the old wooden dairy, and bore its fruit on the leaning side. The main trunk was almost horizontal and couldn't straighten now, so that the heavy, one-sided crop promised by the clusters of tiny green, red-tinged balls, would surely prostrate it altogether.

Louise edged in close to the pile of garden rubbish that her aunt stacked between the tree and the rotted fence. Eva was not a gardener and there were no neat flower-beds, but she was fond of the fuchsias and the grapevine, the plum tree and the mulberry tree—especially the mulberry tree over the out-house—that the old men had planted, and the bulbs and the roses that the old grandmothers had planted. However, she had to cut back the growth sometimes so that they could walk in the small yard and get through the gate.

Louise hid her parcel under the garden rubbish. There was no other house on this side of the cottage but the fence had palings missing in many places, some gaps being as much as a foot wide.

She was just straightening up when she saw the boy. He was passing along the fence, eyeing her through the gaps.

'Hello,' he said.

It was Johnathan Baird who was in the second division of Form IV. Not that he would remain in the second division long. He was smart, and in the second division only because

6

his family had recently moved into the town and he had started at the High School late in the year. The move was due to his father being one of the mine workers put off when the 'Western Hill' deep quartz gold mine, nine miles out, had closed down for good at the beginning of the year. It was not that the gold was worked out, but the price of gold on the world market had not increased in many years, while cost of production had risen steadily, making quartz gold-mining no longer payable.

Everyone knew that Peter Baird had used his savings to buy the declining Corner Store, a small mixed business isolated from the town's main shopping centre. People round about weren't optimistic for him. Locals felt no particular loyalty to support the new-comer, especially as the whole district was feeling the squeeze of bad times on the land. They still went the extra distance to the recently opened, fluorescent-lit supermarket, even though the new store-keeper tried to keep his prices competitive. People seemed to think he would have a struggle to bring up four children, three sons and a daughter, on the takings. Johnathan was the eldest, five years older than his sister, Beth, who was followed by Michael and Andrew.

'Hello,' he repeated, grinning. She stared, wondering if he had seen her hide the parcel.

'Burying the body, eh?'

Louise hadn't spoken often to Johnathan. He was probably the same age, with a tall frame yet to fill out. His face was the narrow, longish Australian face, his blue eyes set back, and his hair a straight no-colour brown. He was quiet but those eyes had lights in them and he smiled easily.

She frowned at him. 'What are *you* doing along our fence?'

'Going fishing.' He waved the rod at her, and she noted that it was a good rod and reel. 'And it may be your fence . . . but this is anyone's paddock.'

It was a wide paddock, tufty with kangaroo grass, that stretched a couple of miles over rise and flat to the line of trees that marked the course of the river. In between, the sweep was broken with two or three small farmhouses, an occasional stand of ironbarks—all that remained of what had been open forest—and scattered, self-propagated plum trees, now in

7

bright spring leaf after blossoming pink and white in early spring. Curving around from the front of the cottage and its two companion cottages was the stretch of diggings which swept first to the right and then back to the left as it followed the depression of the old creek bed across to the river.

'What's in the parcel?' he quizzed her.

Her head tilted; the parcel had nothing to do with him. 'I was looking at the tree. The trunk's nearly on the ground.'

The boy eyed the tree and she remembered she had heard him say once that he hoped to be an orchardist, but that it took money to buy into the good apple country. The orchardist had come after the squatter and the digger but now the overseas apple market had deteriorated and many of the orchards, in turn, were being given over to big companies grazing Herefords. So, looking at Johnathan, Louise thought he was a bit stupid to think of being an orchardist now. He had said that his mother wanted him to be an electrical engineer in this computer age and the practical side of Louise considered this a much more sensible idea. But she had heard, too, about him buying a calf that had been almost dead in a cattle truck, and rearing it to be a good milking cow; and, just lately when sheep from the drought-stricken north had been selling at less than a dollar apiece, he had bought half-a-dozen. You couldn't be interested in computers, she supposed, if you liked cows and sheep and trees.

'You ought to do something about that trunk,' he advised; 'the weight of this year's crop—all on one side—is likely to tear the tree out altogether.'

'But what can we do?'

'You might cut it back to an upright growing limb—give it a fresh start.'

'But it wouldn't be the same tree.' When the tree was bare it was a great spiky spiderweb; when it was thatched with new leaf and fruit it was a green place; when it dropped its yellow leaves in autumn, it dropped gold back into the earth. A cut-back stump with one upright limb like a flag-pole would not be this tree.

'You might try straightening and supporting the trunk a

little—though I don't think you'll get it up very far,' he added.

'It's too heavy for me and Eva to lift.'

'I could bring my father's wheel-jack over one night after school. Maybe I could raise it a bit and you could shove a brick or two under just to stop it keeling over further.'

'I'd like to save it,' she said; 'it's always been here.'

'O.K.—one night through the week. Hoo-roo.'

He went on then, whistling, rod across his shoulder, and didn't look back.

She hadn't seen him with a rod before and wondered why he was going fishing off to the right, away from the river. The fat red-fin, introduced into the river from Europe when grandfather Ed was a boy, and sometimes weighing four or five pounds, were very good eating. But Johnathan was heading towards a rubble-pocked mining gully where a feeding stream only trickled even in the springtime of the year.

CHAPTER TWO

Louise wore the red dress when she left the cottage later in the afternoon. If her aunt were surprised that she made no further protest, that she didn't say again 'I won't wear it!', she gave no sign.

Eva didn't make the mistake of commenting on how well the colour suited the girl, or that it fitted her better than it had fitted Sheila, who was heavier. When Louise was ready to go, she didn't even get up from her chair by the living-room fire, where the newspaper—which they could afford to buy only on Saturday—was scattered on the floor around her in Saturday afternoon half-holiday fashion.

She said, 'Bruce will walk back with you, Lou, if it's dark . . . Mrs Burton told me.'

'I'll leave before dark,' Louise said; 'I don't want Bruce to walk back with me.'

'He's a nice boy.'

'Being the bank manager's son doesn't make him a nice boy.'

'What's wrong with him?'

'Nothing. He's all right.' Louise spoke casually. She didn't know Bruce very well. Until this year, when he had started at the local Technical School, he had been a boarder at a city college; and now, with Sheila away, there wasn't much opportunity for contact, though the girls at school talked about him a lot. He was one for in-gear, already had a heavy chin strap of beard, and was worldly enough to take his pick from

10

the girls. Always talking about things, too; such as how to get rich, or National Service, or apartheid, or his parents. He swore that his parents didn't understand him.

Louise wasn't much interested in any of Bruce's subjects, except perhaps the parents. Most parents, she felt, seemed all right, and Sheila had had no complaints about the ones she shared with Bruce. Of course, as far as she herself was concerned, Eva was difficult. Her aunt had never attempted to improve herself; talked about an article being 'broke' when she should have said 'broken', accepted her life as a cleaner and was always endeavouring to impress on Louise that the cottage was the world. She talked as though they would live forever in the cottage, and die in the cottage, and be buried surely, if it were possible, in the garden of the cottage.

But then Eva wasn't a parent. Perhaps that explained why she had no ambition.

Louise felt, at this moment, that there was no need to tell Eva the stories that went around about Bruce. 'It's just the way you said "nice boy",' she said. 'What you really wanted to say was "he's the *bank manager's* son".'

Without knowing it, Eva pressed hard back into the wooden chair. Louise was very quick, and Eva didn't have the quick words to reply, even if the answers were there. It was the way the young were taught nowadays—to express themselves—to stand up before a class and say what they thought on any subject. Maybe they were a cleverer generation, some people said they were, but Eva thought it was because they had been taught to use words. She didn't think they were cleverer. Only smarter, perhaps, in such a moment as this. Silently she acknowledged the truth of what Louise had just said. Yes, he was the bank manager's son, but she hadn't thought that this made him nice until Louise expressed the thought for her.

Louise was quick. And growing up. Eva had always known, in a nebulous way, that this would happen, that this moment would come. But she hadn't expected a thing like the red dress to mark the moment.

Her thoughts raced to meet the contingency. Perhaps she should sell the Chinese painting on glass now and set the girl

11

up with some clothes. If only she knew if *now* was the time. But surely there were years to get over yet—Louise was still a schoolgirl—and the painting might not bring enough to cover the trend once started. She didn't really know if the painting were valuable or not.

'He's only sixteen,' said Louise cruelly, 'and the Burtons are leaving the district after Christmas—you know that Mr Burton's five-year term is up, don't you?'

'Yes.'

Eva sighed. This time for herself. She would miss Mrs Burton. She was a good woman to work for, always generous, even grateful for the way Eva kept the house and the bank chambers. She would pass her on to the incoming manager's wife with a good reference. But Eva would miss her. She was about her own age, and they had had lots of talks about their children. Mrs Burton had been very helpful in regard to Louise. It was natural that she should know more about children than Eva, having physically produced her own two, Bruce and Sheila, whereas Eva had only come by Louise.

Outwardly Eva accepted this assumption—who was she to disagree with Julia Burton?—and yet she couldn't believe that a real mother could know more of the emotional strain, the anxieties and the joys of caring for baby and child than she had had. She had suffered all things for Louise, plus the added one—insecurity of hold. She wasn't Louise's mother, she was only her aunt. She often lay awake at night, wondering if Louise would abandon her when she was old.

Because of this fear she wished there was some way of binding the girl to her. When the baby had been dependent, it had seemed impossible that the close relationship would be anything but forever. She had given up much for her. Her own life. Perhaps even a child of her own, for Arty Matthews would have married her. But she hid both from the girl—the fear and the desire to possess. She knew that these things would drive Louise from her.

So she didn't get up from the cedar chair, which great-grandfather William, being something also of a joiner and carpenter, had designed and made to fit the fleshy bottom, when Louise said, 'See you,' and went through the kitchen and out the back door.

The most direct way to the bank was not out the back door and through the gate in the back fence. The town lay to the front of the cottage, out-of-sight across the mutilated Ginger Gully where frogs always croaked, unless there was going to be a frost. But Louise had her own reasons for taking the longer way round.

She pushed Millie into the kitchen before banging the door shut. Eva's attention would be taken by the cat and she would move the newspaper for her from the most favoured corner of the hearth mat.

Louise didn't look back to the kitchen as she stopped by the apple tree. She was certain Eva wouldn't rise from her chair to watch her go. Quickly she pulled the parcel from under the garden rubbish and stepped through a hole in the fence.

The spring growth of kangaroo grass was high in the paddock, contrasted here and there with the dark shiny green of daffodil and jonquil clumps—indicating the vanished presence of a cottage and its people—that had borne their golden flowers a month or two ago. But the growth was not lush, for the earth around this mining area was not good productive earth. Between the tufts of grass and gorse, the pebbled surface showed through. The immediate dairy farms were poor, the owners scarcely making a living. The good country was the granite country where the orchards were, seven miles or so over the hills.

Gold had fixed the site of the town. At the height of the rush there had been 30,000 diggers here and fifty pubs. The overall population was 8,000 today and had been for the last fifty years. A solid town, said the Mayor. But a town that hadn't grown in a long time, either.

Louise turned to the right into the rubble-tossed gully and walked quickly, not that she was in a hurry to get to her destination but rather to the sheltered spot on Pelican Flat where she could change the red dress for her own old blue one, wrapped in the newspaper. It was faded and also had a let-down hem, but was her own.

13

She would return home in the blue dress. That would rock Aunt Eva.

The afternoon sun was stronger now and warm on her face. It brightened the red colour. Now and again she glanced down at it and hated it, even though she knew it was a good dress. Too good. People who knew them would know it wasn't hers, that Eva couldn't afford such a dress for her. To advertise that you were on the lowest social rung—an inconsequential segment of this country town—was what hurt. Some day, some how, she would be part of the world. Most of the kids left the place. All those who could manage to get matric got out, went on to university, or training college, or straight into commerce. The ones who stayed were mostly the poor, the apathetic, and those who had to have the security of the familiar.

Yet Louise knew enough of economics to realise that there were probably not as many 'have-nots' in the town now as in Eva's day. Times were more prosperous generally. That was what made being one of the 'have-nots' in a community where more people had more things so much worse. She knew this was why she was so bitter about the red dress. It symbolised her status. That was why she was so bitter towards her aunt— she couldn't understand how Eva could bear to go on living always in the shadow of someone else—the town, the grand- fathers, Julia, even her niece.

As she looked down at the dress she was acutely aware, too, of her knees which she felt were bony and knobbly. Most of the girls in the town were already wearing their dresses to their knees, or mid-calf. Last year she had worn her dresses thigh- high and it hadn't mattered about her knees. But now their ugliness should be covered.

It made it even harder to have to wear this dress, and those two others hanging now in the wardrobe.

To reach the sheltered spot where she was going to change out of the red into the blue meant taking this devious route to the town, and crossing the wasteland humped with the grave- shaped mounds of filled-in shafts towards which Johnathan had headed. She hoped he wouldn't be about.

There were gravelly red dunes now, with some gorse and

Chinese scrub breaking the redness. It was claimed that the Chinese had brought in the shrub-like coffee bush as a seed experiment, but this was not true. The ugly, useless Chinese coffee bush, so-called, and classified as a noxious weed, was an indigenous plant that grew in poor areas. It hadn't been prevalent enough to notice until the diggers had removed the top soil and laid waste the land, giving it a wider area in which to prosper.

Even while she picked her way over the lumpy ground, she was sad for what the gully had once contained—a clear flowing stream, sleek-skinned water-rat and water-fowl, wattles, messmate and redgums on the slopes. And where was the gold now?

Just before she reached the sheltered spot, she heard voices and shouting. When she rounded the knoll she saw the group in the distance. A crowd of youths—five or six, she judged—milling around something on the ground, taking a kick at it, whatever it was, and making funny growling noises in their throats. Animal sort of noises, not proper shouting.

She eased her pace, trying to decide which was the best route to take now to avoid them. To the left perhaps, making the distance further, but she didn't want to pass them in this dress. She knew they would cat-call and whistle.

But it was too late. They had seen her. The red, of course. It stood out like a beacon.

A word from one of them and they all turned, except the thing on the ground. Now she saw that it was another youth lying there. But he was not still for at once he struggled to sit up. The rest stared at her for a second, watching her come. She must have looked like a flame crossing the paddock.

She quickened her pace. For she realised that they had been kicking the one on the ground. She raced towards them like a signal of danger, her anger as burning red as her dress. How dare they! Five or six of them, and one on the ground.

She was not afraid as she ran across the earth that had been shovelled and sifted and shredded until it looked like something regurgitated.

Then one of them broke from the group and headed away from her, away from the others, away from the boy still trying to sit up. The absconder fled on long legs and, suddenly, the others turned too and sprang after him, like cattle panicked by the smell of sudden danger. Contempt speeded her own legs. 'I'm only a girl . . . in a red dress . . . and they run!' She giggled as she wondered whether it was her or the colour they fled from. They ran very fast, scattering as they went, as a gang does from a policeman, so that only one risks being caught.

But she didn't pursue any of them. She stopped when she came to the one on the ground. He was sitting up now, rubbing his head where it had been bumped on the gravel. There were scratches and a gravel graze on one side of his face. As she stopped he ceased rubbing his head to rub the side of his stomach.

'A bloke needs Ned Kelly's armour against boots!'

'Johnathan! What were they doing to you!'

'Having a go at me.'

'Are you hurt?' She bent quickly to inspect his face.

'Not really. The thing had just got going—at ground level, anyway.' He grinned with some satisfaction. 'I got in a few thumps first. Reckon one of them at least will have a black eye.'

'Good for you! Can you get up?'

She would have helped him to his feet but he managed without her.

'You saved me from a bashing,' he said when he stood upright. 'Boots look big as hell when they're coming at you and you're down. Thanks a lot.'

'Don't,' she said, suddenly embarrassed.

He rubbed damp clayey earth from his jeans which were far dirtier than even the fight accounted for. His clothes looked as though he had been engaged in muddy work, not fishing. 'They didn't scare you,' he said, admiringly.

'I hate cowards—people who don't play fair. I hate all kinds of unfairness.'

He saw at once that her thoughts had taken her beyond bashings.

Then she asked. 'Do you know who they were?'

'No. I've seen some of the blokes about—from the Tech, I think. But I don't know any of them.'

16

'Then why . . .?'

'I reckon they think this is their territory. I was trespassing. Mob rule.'

'You'd better not come around this part again.'

He looked at her. 'I've as much right here—or anywhere—as they have.'

'You might get really hurt.'

'They took me by surprise today. I'll never let them corner me again. They're not going to stop me going . . . where I want to go.'

'But why look for trouble, unless there's some special reason?'

He turned away, not answering, and she didn't probe. If he didn't want to talk it was his own business and, no doubt, her opinion didn't count for much.

Then she saw the broken fishing-rod. 'Did they do that?'

'Yeah. Reckon it's a bent pin for a hook and a bit of string for a line from now on.'

'What's your dad going to say?'

'I'll have to tell him I fell on it. Otherwise Mum will worry every time I'm out. And they'll want me to go to the police. Mothers are funny like that.'

'Yeah.'

'Does your mum worry?'

'I haven't got a mum. I've got an aunt.'

'Oh-h . . . Anyway, you came at the right moment, saved me from bruises I'd have to explain away. That's why I'm specially grateful. I won't have to say anything about it at home.'

'Did you catch any fish . . . before . . .?'

'No.'

'Where were you fishing?'

She looked around at the immediate rubbishy country. Here the diggers had pushed the creek hard over to the perpendicular cliff of the red hill they had guillotined sideways, where it trickled silently now through the marsh of bulrushes. This bit of Pelican Flat had been turned over and over, men working so close together that it had been well-nigh impossible not to tunnel from one claim to the next. When the licence tax had been imposed and the police empowered to collect the money,

17

this now empty space had rung with cries of 'The traps are comin'!' or 'Look out for the Joes!' Later, with the arrival of hordes of Chinese, the shouts were 'Keep John Chinaman out! Run 'im off the diggings!' And sometimes in the burning of Chinese canvas camps and stores, the angry, covetous European digger had ripped a Chinese pig-tail out by the roots and hung it on his tent-pole as a trophy.

Now—with those animal-grunting youths gone—the Flat was silent. Louise noted that the seed-pods of the six-foot-tall bulrushes were ready to burst. She had planned to change her dress behind some of those clumps of rushes.

She asked again, 'Where were you fishing?'

But the vague wave of his hand over towards the river, two miles away, told her nothing. She didn't think he had been fishing.

'That dress is a good colour,' he said; 'you . . . sort of . . . look pretty.' He was awkward with his compliment, being unused to making them, but he was sincere. At school, apart from that shining hair, he had never noticed her; she didn't stand out among the other girls, not in looks anyway, or even in the things she did. The red colour gave her more personality than the dull grey of the uniform. 'The dress made them see you coming.'

She was angry at once. 'I hate it! It isn't mine! Sheila's cast-off. Would *you* like to wear someone's cast-off?'

'I always finish off Dad's sports coats.'

'That's different. He's your family. But Sheila's my friend—and my aunt cleans her mother's house. She's given us enough of the damn things for me to wear all summer.'

Louise was so angry that her eyes watered; not that she was given to crying, or even talking of her troubles. Sheila was the only one to whom she had ever confided her close thoughts. They had confided in each other, with never a thought or an experience not shared. But because Louise couldn't match Sheila's experiences, she had opened up the inner recesses of her mind to her friend. Sheila had laughed sometimes at where her imagination led, but she had always understood. Because of Sheila she had never found it necessary to talk to Eva, and now

18

there was no one with whom to talk. She had plenty of friends at school, but no one to whom she confided. There could be only one Sheila. But sometimes she wondered if Sheila were having this same cut-off experience, or whether she had found another close friend at the boarding-school. Sometimes in her letters Sheila mentioned new friends. It would be natural for her to do this, going amongst a new set of people, but Louise couldn't find another mate amongst girls with whom she had grown up but never allowed into her confidence.

So it was strange and unusual to find herself talking to Johnathan, and yet so easy. She had never suspected that a boy might be easy to talk to. Looking at him, she thought he suited earth on his hands, and a fishing rod. But he should have a dog. Johnathan and a dog should be one. Then she remembered hearing something of the disappearance of his dog—a good kelpie—picked up by a passing truckie, someone said.

'I'm not going to stay in this town all the summer, and wear those dresses,' she told him.

'But if Sheila's your friend . . . ?'

'Don't you see!—that makes it worse!' Louise didn't add that the one tarnished link in that friendship had been the fact that Eva had been grateful to Mrs Burton for Sheila being her friend—as though it were a special favour. Not that she and Sheila had let this worry them, for their friendship had been of their own choosing and their own making. But even before Sheila left, Louise had been often irritated by her aunt's attitude.

'I'm going to the city soon,' she declared; 'as soon as I can leave without being in strife for not attending school the required number of days for the year. I'll get a job for the summer holidays. I can work in a shop or a factory . . . anything.'

'What'll your aunt say? She'll stop you, won't she?'

'I won't let her stop me! She's not my mother—she didn't have me.'

Johnathan continued to rub the clayey mud from his clothes while he considered the girl and her words. No girl—no

19

strange girl—had ever confided in him before. His sister Beth told him things sometimes—her thoughts—but they were a child's thoughts and never demanded more than he was already equipped to give. No doubt this was the sort of thing men and women did—talked over their problems. He felt mature and knowledgeable and conscious of his sex, especially when she asked him, with wide eyes, 'How do you think I should go about it, Johnathan?' She was asking his advice. For the first time in his life he could have reached out and touched her because she was a girl. But he was still honest. 'I don't know. I don't know whether you should even leave home.'

'I have to leave home. That's the one thing I do know.'

'Have you got enough money for your fare? Enough to pay your board till you get your first pay?'

'No more than a few dollars. But I wouldn't have to pay my board in advance, would I? The landlord would wait a week, wouldn't he?' Now Louise was being feminine. She wanted him to tell her what she already knew.

'You mightn't get a job straight off. Thousands of kids go after jobs in the Christmas holidays.'

'I know.'

'You might run into some trouble loose on your own. You don't know the city.'

Johnathan didn't know the city himself. But he read the newspapers and knew what could happen to young, inexperienced girls.

He felt an insistence now to help, lead, even to dominate, to protect her from these hazards.

Louise sighed bleakly. She knew she would be frightened when she stepped off the train in the city, but she would go just the same. The fear of the city would be less to bear than the humiliation of wearing those dresses in the town.

'You'll need money to tide you over that first week or two,' he said decidedly.

She was glad he was definite. It made her decision to take the Chinese painting on glass a right one. There was no other way she knew of obtaining money. And Eva hadn't looked at

20

the painting for a long time. In fact, Eva's mother had brought Eva up to be somewhat ashamed of possessing the painting. Eva's mother had been a woman of strict principles, and an abhorrence of the 'pagan idolators' who sought the favour and direction of the idol Joss with presents of oil, tea and opium. At the same time she was a thrifty woman who, on Sundays, had sent Eva across the paddock to Wang Lou, a Chinese digger turned market-gardener, for a tuppeny lettuce; and at Christmas had allowed Eva to keep the gifts of box-kites he made, with wonderful Chinese dragons painted on the sides. The result was that Eva didn't like to take the offending painting to the rubbish dump—after all Wang Lou had been very nice, and the painting *had* belonged to great-grandfather William—nor did she like to sell it openly because people would ask how she came by it. And Eva didn't tell lies.

The fact was—as grandmother had claimed—great-grand-father had stolen it! (Not that Eva expressed it that way.) Pinched the jolly thing from the shanty home of Chan Ah-Foo. After the old Chinese had died, of course, and not likely to want to look at it any more.

Great-grandfather William had just happened to be passing the Chinaman's shanty, and hearing the squeak of the door as it swung in the evening wind, had peeked in, and there was old Chan Ah-Foo, all huddled up on his bunk, his opium pipe at his side, quite dead. 'But smiling . . . happy like,' Eva always added when she told the tale.

Great-grandfather had 'removed' some of the Chinaman's things, such as jars of Canton ginger and Joss sticks and the painting, 'for safety', Eva said. With so many dishonest men on the goldfields great-grandfather had considered the matter, and done what he thought best. After all, Chan Ah-Foo might have relatives in China, who would come or send for his belong-ings, so great-grandfather had decided to keep them safe until they came. He had gone back to the shanty, when it was quite dark, of course, so that no one would see him carry the things to safety, especially other Chinese men. No European would remonstrate; except to regret that he hadn't been first to hear the squeaking door.

Now there were no Chinese in the town, but his grand-daughter still had the painting.

To remove it, sell it in the city, would surely remove an embarrassment from Eva, Louise rationalised. Carrying it to the city and finding a buyer would be the difficult part. A painting on glass was a fragile thing.

At this point, Louise didn't feel it necessary to tell Johnathan about the painting.

'It's a matter you should think over very well,' Johnathan cautioned.

'I've thought enough—I couldn't bear to stay in this town over the summer.'

'Do you want me to think about it, too—and let you know if I come up with any ideas?'

'I certainly would.' It was comforting to have Johnathan to talk to. She hadn't opened out to anyone since Sheila had gone.

'Louise . . .' Johnathan smiled, although his grazed face twinged, 'you helped me today—I'd like to help you, if you want me.'

Louise clutched her newspaper parcel tighter. 'I appreciate that,' she said, 'I'll need some help.'

'And about the apple tree—I'll come in the morning, seeing it's Sunday.'

'Thanks,' she said, and turned and set off over the uneven ground into the tall rushes but her step, though still quick, was no longer tense. She walked with almost a jaunty air.

CHAPTER THREE

The town was quiet on a Saturday afternoon. After the scramble of Saturday morning shopping the stores closed and, except for litter on the footpaths and in the gutters, dogs scrounging, and vehicles still parked outside hotels, the streets were deserted.

When not obscured by people, you could see the gold town, with its several century-old stone banking premises, built to transact the business of a great inland city which had failed to remain great; its equally imposing town hall and government offices and its many wide-balconied hotels, most of which were no longer in business. A gold town, in fact, from which the gold had long been taken.

The bank where Dan Burton was manager was in the main street, and the bank residence was part of the two-storey business premises, with a high fence screening the private garden at the side. The building was of grey granite quarried in the district, with a roof of local grey slate, and there were protective grills of fine wrought-iron lace enclosing the lower half of the upper floor windows.

At the side of the bank chambers there was an iron-lace gate which led to the private side entrance, and Louise knew that it would be unlocked in readiness for her. She had often come here to Saturday tea when Sheila had been home, and stayed the rest of the week-end.

Before opening the gate, she smoothed her blue dress over her thighs and straightened the collar. She wondered if Mrs

Burton would be expecting to see the red dress, as the woollen material was just right for this in-between-seasons weather. Whatever she was expecting, she was the kind of woman who knew exactly what to say and do to suit the moment. Louise had learned a lot of her manners from watching her friend's mother.

The small garden inside the high stone fence was very neat with primulas in bloom edging the square of green lawn, roses espaliered on the walls and the shrubs beautifully controlled. Mrs Burton did the garden herself, wearing dark glasses and a big hat when she worked outdoors.

The entrance to the residence was set in the middle of the side wall of the building, with four stone steps leading up to the door. Julia Burton answered the door bell herself.

'Come in, Louise,' she said, welcoming her with a kiss. 'Do you know it's at least two months since you were here, and Sheila is constantly asking for first-hand reports of you. Come in.'

But, somehow, the girl saw that Sheila's mother *had* been expecting the red dress.

Julia took the girl into the lounge room, with its green brocade-upholstered couch and arm-chairs, thick-piled green carpet against cream-painted walls and floral cushions. There was no goldfields bric-a-brac here. A magnificent eighteenth-century *cloisonné* vase at one end of the marble mantel-piece, a *Sèvres* shepherdess at the other, and a pair of Chippendale mahogany chairs, one on either side of the couch, revealed, without the need for emphasis, that the Burtons knew their antiques.

Louise admired Julia Burton's taste. She liked the way the woman wore her dark hair swept up and then around to one side of her face; the smooth, pale skin, the deep blue eyes, the straight nose and the tall figure with the fine waist-line. Louise knew the word for Julia—elegant. Not like Eva who disguised her bulky figure in the straight shifts she wore.

'Bruce is having a shower,' his mother said. 'He took his panning dish and went specking with some of his mates this afternoon. He usually does quite well—though I'm always telling him that some of the old jars and bottles that were thrown away by the diggers are more valuable today than the specks of gold.'

Louise nodded. She knew that Julia, as well as Dan, was an authority on such matters. Their collection, which ranged from a blue castor-oil bottle to the much-coveted 'bullet' lemonade bottle, was kept, appropriately, in the bank cellar.

'All he got this afternoon, however, was a black eye . . . the result of a fall,' his mother went on. 'Sometimes I think boys should only be allowed out on a leash. Bringing up a son, Louise, is a complicated process.' Julia sighed; she knew that Bruce was going his own way and that neither she nor Dan had much say any more. 'Sheila's never been any trouble. I suppose you miss her as much as I do.'

'Yes,' Louise missed her more when she came to this house because if Sheila had been at home, she and Louise would have been in her bedroom, talking . . . talking . . . talking . . . of the things girls talk about, even about boys for Sheila had been very interested in boys last year. More so than Louise who now hoped that Mrs Burton wouldn't ask her if the dress fitted, or whether she liked it. One of the things she hadn't learned was the polite lie; yet truth sometimes prickled.

'You didn't come very early,' Julia complained, 'I was hoping for a long talk—maybe to hear what you're going to do next year. Eva says you still don't know what you want to be?'

'No, Mrs Burton.'

'And to hear what you've been doing lately—how school is going. But we'll soon have to have tea because I promised Eva I wouldn't keep you late.'

'Yes,' said Louise, remembering that Eva never spoke of Mrs Burton as Julia. But it was Eva she was angry with, not Julia—how could Eva have so little ambition, so little pride? On Monday she would be the cleaner in this room. She felt her face getting hot and the chair no longer comfortable.

Then Bruce came in. He was a tall sixteen-year-old with broad shoulders, almost a man in build, except that he was still a bit loose-limbed. He had the same colouring as his mother, with the same good features cast in a masculine mould. His

25

hair was wet from the shower and sleek flat to his head but he had rubbed his beard dry and it fuzzed across his chin. He hadn't had to make a choice between long or short hair, because at the Tech—like the High School—hair past the collar was taboo.

Louise knew from Sheila why he had been taken from the city college and enrolled at the local Technical School. For the last two years his exam results had been extremely poor, and the principal of the city college had suggested that Bruce might do better under the parental eye. The boy was above average intelligence but was not using it, the report said. He had no idea of what he wanted to be, but it seemed that his talents might run to some kind of engineering, or some work to do with his hands, inventive or creative.

But Bruce had been displeased with the change and, up-to-date, his term results had not improved. In her letters, Sheila had told Louise that he was a great disappointment to their parents.

He was good-looking and walked arrogantly because he knew girls found him good-looking; even the cut above his eye didn't detract from his confidence.

Louise saw that the skin around his eye was black and yellow. He must have fallen very heavily.

'He struck a sharp edge of slate,' his mother said.

Bruce was staring back at Louise, but at her dress rather than at her face. 'A blue dress . . . eh?' he said.

Louise coloured, until she heard the echo of puzzlement in his voice. Then she suddenly remembered the long legs fleeing away from her across the flat, and the rest of the boys scattering. She should have recognised him then! Should have recognised all of them! Not that she knew them very well. They were boys from the Technical School, and she knew them only because she had seen them around with Bruce.

Bruce had led the field away from the boy on the ground; but he had not had a panning dish in his hand as he ran, nor had any of the others.

She almost said 'It was *you!*' but, in time, she remembered Julia. There were things from which you had to protect a mother and, in any case, she would have had to say that the red dress, at the moment, was wrapped in newspaper and lying behind a clump of bulrushes.

Instead she asked 'Does it hurt?' and hoped that it did.

'Not now—though the slate was a bit sharp.'

'I'm sure it was.'

Bruce didn't notice the sarcasm. He was at ease again. He didn't think now that it was she who had run across the paddock—a possibility, at the time that had really set him moving. Changing her dress had tricked him and he felt safe from her knowing.

'I'll put on a record while Mum's doing things about the tea.'

The player was a handsome polished instrument with radio as well.

'Can you dance?' he asked.

'No,' said Louise.

He was surprised. All the girls of her age in the city could dance and he'd been invited to many parties. 'I'll teach you.'

Louise stood quite still. She didn't want Bruce to teach her to dance, not after seeing him kick and run. It was a picture of him that would remain in her mind and she was sorry, for she felt she should like Sheila's brother.

'Your High School dance is next Friday,' he said; 'it won't be much fun for you if you can't dance. I'm going. One of the girls in the sixth invited me to be her partner. But I'll give you some dances. Come on—let's try this one.'

The rhythm of the music was deep and exciting, so that it was hard not to sway to its beat. He moved towards her and tried to draw her forward with an arm around her shoulders. 'Like this . . .'

But she pulled away. 'I know a bit . . . enough. I can dance all I want. You don't have to teach me.'

He stepped back, and his cut eye twitched. 'Who are you going with?'

'Johnathan Baird,' she said, and stared at the yellowing eye. Johnathan hadn't asked her; in fact no one had asked her. She felt she knew why. Funny knees put boys off. A boy would never admit it, but the first girl he took out must be near perfect, at least in his eyes. She must wear a dress that would draw some admiration from his mates, or at least raise no criticism, and she should belong, preferably, to parents who had a business or a farm; in short the very normal. Except, of course, for those boys who liked the really way-out. But those boys didn't appeal to her, anyway.

And she didn't appeal to the others, she thought. It was not so small a town that everybody knew everybody else, but there were layers of society and although sometimes the layers over-lapped at the edges, the main strata remained undisturbed. You were known by the company you kept; and her father had left her mother and her aunt was a cleaner. No real discrimina-tion—it was just at this age most boys preferred not to be conspicuous. In a couple of years the same boys would seek her. She realised she might have got over the difficulty now by burying it herself, by believing in herself, but she couldn't. It stayed with her.

'*If* I go . . .' she added, pushing the long hair out of her eyes, and controlling her body that wanted to sway with the music.

'If . . .? Haven't really made up your mind then?'

'Not yet.'

'I know that Johnathan Baird fellow . . . by sight. Moved into town recently, didn't he? Father's got the Corner Store?'

'Yes.'

'He'll tread on your toes, I bet!'

'He's good,' said Louise, having never danced with Johnathan, or known him even really until today. She wasn't even sure that he danced.

Bruce switched off the player. Obviously he considered the music wasted on this girl, or perhaps he was wondering why she had named Johnathan Baird as her partner 'if she went'.

Then Julia said tea was ready and they went into the dining-room. It was a high-ceilinged room like the lounge, with similar green carpet, lace dinner mats on the table, and shining silver. The cutlery was heavy and old-fashioned, having belonged to Julia's grandmother. Eva always spoke admiringly of the Burton silver after silver-cleaning day.

Louise had admired it herself until this evening, associating the fine cutlery with Sheila's mother. She had always taken note how the table was set, and watched the way Sheila's mother used knife and fork so that she would learn her way. But tonight she could only remember that Eva had polished the silver yesterday.

Dan Burton was a stocky man, not shorter than his wife but appearing so because of his squareness. He knew his job, everyone said, a great man with figures, and economics, who understood the trend of the times. You could rely on Dan Burton to give you the best deal possible, provided you didn't importune him. Even the most landed farmer knew that when Dan Burton said he was to reduce his overdraft, he had to reduce it. He was a man of influence in the town, as well as being president of the Historical Society, a member of the Progress Association, and an active Rotarian.

He sat at the head of his table. 'That's a fine eye you've got,' he told his son; 'lucky you didn't have to have a stitch.'

'It's nothing,' said Bruce.

'You look as though you've been in a fight.'

'I can't help what you think it looks like.'

'Are you sure it wasn't a fight—not a fall?'

'It was a fall,' said Bruce, his tone as decided as his father's.

Dan Burton started on his soup. Louise saw that a head for figures, an understanding of the monetary trends, a finesse in dealing with the bank's clients, even a solid frame and a confidence in his own judgment, did not bridge the gap between Dan Burton and his son. Louise didn't know Bruce very well, but she knew more about him than did his father.

Mr Burton, it turned out, had heard there was a Chinese visitor to the town and this led to a discussion—mainly conducted by Dan himself—on why the Chinese men of the gold-rush days had come to Australia without their wives, at a time when there was no restriction on the entry into Australia of Chinese women.

'There were three reasons, I think,' Dan said; 'firstly, it was the duty of Chinese women to remain home to look after the parents, grandparents and children; secondly, Chinese women whose feet had been bound could not totter about the deck of a lurching sailing-ship; and thirdly, the cost of the fare, which was £5 from Canton, was a lot of money to a Chinese peasant.'

'And pretty awful travelling,' ventured Louise, realising that Bruce was bored by the subject, and would be amused that she found it interesting. He would probably write her off as a square head.

'It was a racket for the shipping companies,' Dan said. 'They used the lure of the gold to fill their holds with human cargo—like a herd of cattle between decks. That £5 was nearly all profit for the shippers—the poor devils even had to supply their own food and bedding.'

'Just shows what we'll suffer—even Chinamen—for gold or money,' Bruce tossed in airily, while giving Louise a knowing nudge under the table on her big toe. He hurt her toe, and she returned with a kick on the bony knob of his ankle.

'There were forty thousand of them on this field at the height of the rush,' said Dan, unaware of the under-table exchange; 'and the European diggers were soon complaining that the Chinese were undesirable competitors in the struggle for existence, that wages for labour would drop to the level of slave wages, and that the country would soon be swamped with yellow men. As a result the Government of Victoria decided to levy a poll tax of £10 a head, and forbade ships to land more than one Chinese for every ten tons of their ship's burden.'

'We *do* know our history—if you want to learn anything,' Bruce told Louise, with a sage cock of the head.

'That applied only to Victoria, didn't it, Mr Burton,' Louise said, wriggling her big toe and knowing she was annoying Bruce by extending the topic. 'And lots of them were put ashore at Robe in South Australia and had to walk the three hundred miles from there to the goldfields?'

'Yes—many evaded the tax that way. But it did reduce the numbers coming in. Otherwise . . .' he mused, 'the whole picture of Australia—its way of government and its way of life—would have been drastically different. Even so, the Chinese continued to come with each new discovery of gold until, at the turn of the century, the Commonwealth Government passed a law prohibiting the entry of non-European migrants into Australia. This became known as the "White Australia Policy".'

Bruce prodded Louise's big toe so hard that she was surprised her jump was not noticed. At the same time Bruce waved his fork at his father. 'A fine address, Mr Burton,' he mocked; 'a fine address indeed—history and choice of words—worthy of any Rotarians' after-dinner speaker. But you forgot one thing, Mr Burton—you're at home now.'

'Bruce!' Julia was bringing plates in from the kitchen.

'Well—let's face it—we know Dad can talk. But do we have to have it *every* meal!'

Which made Dan Burton's face darken, but didn't take his attention from the steak which Julia had placed in front of him.

Louise surmised that this restraint was due to her presence. Dan was too disciplined and fastidious to brawl with his son in public. But Louise wished that her leg was long enough to kick Bruce hard, not only for her toe, but for Dan.

She would like to have asked this knowledgeable man—and his wife—what they thought a Chinese painting on glass was worth today but felt that they might, in turn, ask why she was interested. Or Bruce would. In any case, it would get back to Eva, during that morning-tea break which employer and employee shared, that Louise had been talking about her great-grandfather William's painting on glass. So she kept quiet.

31

CHAPTER FOUR

Louise left the bank with ample time to reach home before
dark, declining Julia's offer of her son's company, which
fortunately he backed up without warmth. Even if she'd
wanted, she couldn't have had him, walk home with her on
account of having to pick up the red dress and, anyway, he
had hurt her big toe.

She walked quickly through the still-quiet business section
of the town and out past the houses until she came to the rough
country that she had crossed earlier, then she went more slowly.
She had to watch out for the particular clump of bulrushes
behind which she had left the dress. She didn't really want to
take the dress home or care what happened to it, except that
if someone discovered it, it might be embarrassing for Mrs
Burton.

She found it easily enough although well-hidden under the
sloughed-off layers of the bulrushes. It was wrapped in the
newspaper in which she had carried the blue dress, and now
she tucked the parcel under her arm.

A bit further on, from the top of a yellow-red mound, she
saw Johnathan evidently on his way home. She wondered
where he had been in the meantime. Johnathan hadn't noticed
her and she didn't call out to him. She had her own thoughts,
but she did notice that he was carrying the two pieces of the
broken fishing-rod, and nothing else. If he had been fishing—
and where?—he hadn't caught anything. Bit of a loner, this

Johnathan—perhaps a little like herself. And he would be very late for his tea . . . wouldn't that cause his mother to ask questions?

Tomorrow she would tell him about Bruce's black eye. Or should she? Sheila might not like her telling tales about her brother and, after all, it was only her own suspicion that Bruce was the one who had led the retreat. But she did decide in that moment that she would ask Johnathan to be her partner for the dance. If she didn't turn up with Johnathan, Bruce would know she had lied and would laugh at her.

Johnathan was walking quickly now and by the time she reached the back fence of the cottage he had disappeared.

She didn't feel very pleased with the way of things as she walked up the slate path to the back door, in her blue dress, knowing that there was an issue ahead.

She opened the door and felt the cottage warmth on her cold cheeks. She held the parcel tighter, aware that a corner of the newspaper had ripped, and red flashed forth as bright as a letterbox.

Eva spoke as soon as the door banged. 'You're early . . . I thought you'd stay much longer and walk home with Bruce.'

Louise came through the kitchen and stood before her. She noted that Eva had eaten her Saturday tea of crumpets alone by the living-room fire, as they usually did on Saturday during the cold months. It was one of the small, comfortable things they did together—to abandon the table and sit close to the warmth, Millie resentful if she had to make way on the mat.

Now Eva looked up from her knitting, having tired of the newspaper a long time ago. At first she just stared, not believing. Louise knew why she didn't believe. She had never defied her aunt like this before.

'What have you done with it! Where have you been?'

Louise thrust the parcel towards her and the red glinted.

'I've been to the bank. I didn't wear the dress. I told you I wouldn't wear it.'

Eva stood up as though she had to face Louise at her own level. Her face was round, with very dark grey eyes and her hair was short over her head and ears. She trimmed her hair herself and as there was a wave in it, she never did more than comb it through.

'You didn't wear the dress! Mrs Burton didn't see you in it!'

'No. I changed in the bushes on Pelican Flat. And you needn't look scandalised because no one saw me.'

Eva wasn't looking scandalised, only uncomprehending. Where or how Louise had changed the dress was unimportant; the important thing was that she had not worn the red dress to the bank, although she had left the house in it. That was the frightening part. Before the girl went out she had been prepared to do battle with her, but then Louise had left calmly, with the dress on, and Eva had enjoyed the rest of the afternoon, getting very hot by the fire and even making some toffee of sugar and water in the old saucepan. Louise liked this toffee; she had made it for Louise.

'I can't understand you!' It was a cry. Louise had deceived her, lied to her, by leaving the house wearing the dress. All of a sudden nothing was safe any more—not even honesty. Years ago, at a picnic, she had been taken out in a boat on the river, and someone in devilish fun had pulled out the spigot. She remembered the water rushing in . . . and she couldn't swim. Though why should she think of that swamped boat now? What connection did it have with the fact that her sister's child was no longer a baby, no longer a child that she worked to feed and clothe and keep housed, but a person confronting her who was unaware that she had done any of these things.

'I can't understand *you!*' Louise said. 'Just content to go on in this place—cleaning the bank chambers and residence. How long have you been doing that?—all of your life!'

Eva could have said 'ever since I got you.'

'And picking apples and pears in season! Surely you could have done something different! So that—if we had to stay in this town—at least we would have amounted to something.'

Amounted to something! You were what you were, Eva had always considered, with paying your way and keeping out of debt very important. It kept you poor to pay your debts, her father and grandfather had always said, but you could sleep at night. As for doing some different job—she didn't know anything else. There had never been any thought of her attending school beyond the leaving age of fourteen—as it was then—and certainly no possibility of her going to the city where she might have worked in a factory, so she had started almost immediately to do housework. Beginning with one of the store-keepers' houses and graduating to the bank chambers.

They faced each other—the climax to their first confrontation.

Louise had never been a naughty child, Eva thought wonderingly, and when she had misbehaved a bit of a slap had generally set her right. But you couldn't slap a girl almost as big as a woman, though it was a temptation. She would never slap her again. It had to be words now . . . and Eva was at a disadvantage.

'You'll wear those dresses,' she said, 'they're a godsend, and you know it. There's the roof to be fixed this summer—it's leaked for the last three winters.'

'This cottage is ready for a demolition order!' said Louise viciously.

'There's the roof to be fixed this summer,' Eva repeated, 'and that costs money. Costs money to have a home. But a home is the most important thing you can have . . . my parents taught me.'

Eva had indeed been brought up on stories of the end of the 'land boom' of the '90s when there had been soup kitchens in the town to feed the hungry; and the 'depression' of the '30s when grandfather Ed had been out of work for two years, but slept in a bed at night because the cottage was his own. This latter happy state being due entirely to great-grandmother, widow of William, who had washed and ironed and scrubbed and saved to buy, for a few pounds, the freehold from the Crown of this bit of land over which William had taken out a Miner's Right and on which his cottage stood. Great-grandmother had bought safety of roof for herself and her family.

'If you have a roof, you're safe. You can always get a bit of tucker somewhere—even if you grow a few veges and keep a few chooks.'

But Louise said, 'I'm going to work in the city all the holidays. I'll get some kind of job—in a shop or something.'

Her aunt stared at her.

'I'll stay away until school starts again—I'll come back with a *new* dress.' She didn't say that she might never come back.

'You won't leave this house!' Eva's face was scarlet.

Louise's shoulder lifted, angry with herself. She hadn't meant to come out with her intentions at this stage—with the time of her going not yet fixed—knowing that it would give Aunt Eva time to work out a counter policy, to try, somehow, to stop her. And whatever happened she couldn't stay in the town over the summer.

She turned away abruptly towards her own room, a very small room off the kitchen. The plan of the stone cottage was no plan; just one room growing out of the other as the family had required.

Her furniture was a single iron bedstead and a cedar dressing-table that great-grandfather had made himself, with a small separate mirror on a swivel. Louise was always wishing that the mirror was full-length so that she could see her ridiculous knees.

She threw the red dress in its newspaper covering under the bed, and wondered then what she would do for the rest of the night until bed-time, almost wishing she had stayed at the bank and had Bruce teach her some of the steps she didn't know. Girls in her class would be envious of her chance if they knew.

She couldn't settle to read, even though she loved books and always had school library books at home; she couldn't sit in her room for the walls were suddenly pressing in on her and, in any case, she and Eva couldn't go on being at loggerheads. They had to live together until she went to town. She could hear Eva moving about in the living-room, poking at the fire, and the sounds suggested that she was putting the spark-screen in front of the blaze. But surely she wouldn't be going to bed yet?

She came out of her room to see her aunt about to open the

kitchen outer door. She had her coat on—the dark brown coat that was the only one Louise could ever remember her wearing— and a green scarf tied tightly around her head and face, bulging her cheeks as though she had toothache.

She half-turned as Louise appeared, and her eyes were red with rubbing, or anger.

'I'm going out,' she said, and the door closed after her.

Never before had her aunt left her alone after dark, not because Louise was afraid of the dark, but because Eva believed that a child should not be left alone at night. So this was a milestone, an acknowledgement of a status of growth achieved—old enough to be left alone at night. Louise went into the living-room and removed the screen from the fire, put on more wood and settled to wait for her aunt to return.

CHAPTER FIVE

Louise took off her shoes and sat on the hearth mat which, like the lino in the kitchen, had had its colour and pattern worn off long ago. With her legs bent under her, she stared at the flames of yellow and blue and red—colour sprites released from the wood that sprang to life in the toothless mouth of the chimney. There was company in the sprites and the colour, and she piled the wood high.

The wood was good burning grey-box, some that Eva had bought from Johnathan who, through his father, had a house-licence to cut wood in the State forest. It was permissible to sell any excess over their household requirements. Johnathan sold his wood a little cheaper than anyone else which meant that he never had any on his hands, and indicated sound business judgment. He was a mixture, this Johnathan, thought Louise, with his plans for being a man on the land, yet understanding the value of earning a dollar.

And that led her to think of the city where she would earn a dollar, too. Sitting there, staring at the flames, thinking of the dollar, she realised that tonight was her night of opportunity. She had the house to herself. What better time to take the painting from the top of her aunt's wardrobe? She could lock both front and back doors so that if Eva returned before she had completed the operation she would have time to compose both herself and the house before she opened the door. Eva seldom locked the doors at night but as this was Louise's first night alone, there was surely some excuse for her to do so.

She let Millie in before she turned the key in the back lock, and the cat ran in ahead of her to the fire, heavy of body, yet tail erect as a post. Then Louise went into her aunt's bedroom.

It was a narrow room, sharing half of the front of the cottage with the living-room, and also sharing the chimney on the middle dividing wall, which was eighteen inches thick. The door was at the inner side of the fireplaces.

A double bed with brass bed-posts and fancy rails and knobs was pushed hard into the corner under the small casement window. The bed had stood there since great-grandfather William's day. He had bought it at a time when the creek gold had been yielding better than usual, obviously having an eye for possessions and also the shiny.

Around the walls were many family photographs, including one of William as a bridegroom, and his bride. The bride wore a gown of some stiffened material that hid everything but the shape of her face—her neck being swathed in a choker band—and the tips of her fingers. She was probably seventeen, but looked as a prospective great-grandmother should look. The bridegroom wore a flowered waistcoat and magnificent whiskers, and his eyes looked at you. Funny thing that, about old photographs—they had real eyes.

The tall cedar wardrobe, which was another example of his woodwork, was just inside the door almost hiding from sight everything else in the room.

Louise brought a wooden chair from the kitchen and an old footstool from under the living-room table. To reach the top of the wardrobe she had to put the stool on the chair and stand on top of both. The brass posts of the bed were close enough to help her reach the position, but the stool and the chair rocked when she stood on top because the floor stumps had rotted in places and the floor was uneven. To steady herself she clutched the fancy wooden railing that hid the tray top of the wardrobe.

Her fingers groped over the railing to the layer of newspaper that she knew covered the painting. Eva renewed this cover now and again, though sometimes with a year between, but she hadn't disturbed the painting itself for some time.

Louise's fingers encountered fluff and dust. She tried to

shift this layer of newspaper without actually lifting it off. She wanted to slide the painting, also wrapped in newspaper, from underneath and leave the top layer intact. The less she disturbed the set-up the better. It would be long enough before Eva took the painting from its lodging-place, and unless she actually felt for the glass when she renewed the top layer of newspaper, she would not notice it had been removed.

Great-grandfather must have been quite a boy, Louise reflected, as she balanced on the stool, and if he had lived long enough might have amounted to something in the town. She thought he would have chuckled to see his great-grand-daughter removing the painting, even as he had 're-moved' it from Chan Ah-Foo. Nevertheless, she carefully avoided his watching eyes as, holding the painting in one hand, she used the other to support herself on the bed as she climbed down from stool and chair. She leaned the flat newspaper parcel against the bed as she returned up her improvised ladder to put the dusty cover of paper back in position.

Then she carried the painting into the living-room and sat down again on the hearth rug, while Millie stretched, jealous of her section of the mat. Behind Louise on the table the lamp-flame spluttered as she took off the wrapping, as though someone passed by and created a draught. But there was no one passing by and all the windows were closed for the night was cold, and she had locked the front and back doors. Louise thought she must have breathed hard after the exertion of climbing up and down. Or was Chan Ah-Foo annoyed at being removed?

She tore off the wrappings eagerly, wondering if she would be able to tell if the painting were of any value. Two silverfish ran out as she opened the paper and scuttled under the wood on the hearth. She should have killed them because they ate white patterns into the covers and bindings of her school books, destroying the new look which she loved and always tried to preserve, but she was too eager to get to the painting. She could scarcely remember what it was like, it was so long since she had seen it.

Unwrapped, she lay it on the floor and knelt above it. It was about two feet long and eighteen inches wide, and there was a black, wooden frame around it on a wooden backing. Written on the wooden back were some Chinese characters—perhaps the artist's name—and the word Canton in English. The frame was chipped and looked old and tatty, but not the painting. There it was, a magnificence of intricate design and story. Chinese figures and landscape in fine detail. She knew something of the legend depicted in the picture, though she feared it could be a garbled version. It was what Eva remembered of the story Wang Lou, the market-gardener, had told her as a child, and which she, Louise, had embellished.

The picture showed seven damsels with their feet hidden in the softness of white cloud indicating that they were the Seven Heavenly Maidens that men of the earth knew as the Seven Sisters of the night skies. The Celestial River—the Milky Way—swung its arc across the centre of the picture and there were six Sisters on one side and the Seventh on the other. The latter was clasping her lover the Cowherd. The Seventh Sister had fallen in love with this lowly mortal and, once each year, on the seventh day of the seventh month, she was permitted to cross the Milky Way and declare her love.

It was a romantic story told with the use of the whole spectrum of colour, in warm tones yet as soft and delicate as it was sharp and distinct. But the story finished with that yearly meeting beside the 'River Across the Sky'.

The girl's eyes gathered in the colour and her mind carried the gentle tale further to a happy ending. What did it matter that the maid was heavenly and the cowherd one with the earth? Stories were meant to be like that. One day she would write her own version of the Seventh Sister.

Then the lamplight guttered again and picked out the warm reds, like the red of the dress—why did she have to think of the dress!—and the yellow that reminded her of the gold of the gullies which, in turn, reminded her that the story was only a painting on glass. The marvel being that it was painted on the *inside* of the glass, with the artist seemingly working back to front, yet perfect in the most minute detail.

Louise marvelled at the perfection of figure and landscape that could be achieved by this inside-out method.

She knelt on the mat for a long time and the firelight

polished the gold of her own hair as it hung around and over her face.

Now and again in the stillness the cottage creaked, as though its stumps had rheumatism. The cottage did not often whinge. *Or was Chan Ah-Foo watching and listening?*

She remembered then to go and take the chair from the bedroom and return it to the kitchen and put the footstool back in its spot under the table. She looked carefully about her aunt's bedroom, making sure she had left no trace of her presence.

As she bent to blow out the bedroom lamp the flame caught the rich brass of the bed-posts. When she was very young and had been a little afraid of the dark, Eva had let her sleep with her sometimes, and always the last thing she saw as Eva blew out the lamp was the shine of the bed knobs.

She hoped Eva would not return before the lamp had had time to cool; and was immediately irritated to think that their cottage was one of the few remaining without electric light, because Eva couldn't afford to have it connected.

Then she went back to look at the painting. But only for a moment, and to think 'It is beautiful—it should be worth something. Surely at least my fare to the city and board for the first week.'

She wrapped it up again very carefully, and tied the newspaper with string. She had already decided that until she was ready to take it to town, she would hide it under the house. There was a vent opening along the side, screened by a fuchsia bush, which she had always used for a hide-away for the things she did not show to Eva, like bits of poetry she wrote, and once a short story. There was nothing under there at the moment because recently, in great dissatisfaction with what she had written, she had burned the pieces.

The opening was just a narrow space to allow air to enter between the floor boards and the ground, the cottage having been built close to the earth, but it was quite dry underneath and the painting would be there such a short time that it could come to no harm.

She picked up the parcel and walked through the doorway

into the kitchen and across to the back door. She carried the parcel carefully; it weighed a few pounds but was more awkward than heavy. The lamp was not lit in the kitchen but there was sufficient light coming from the living-room and she could open the door, even the locked door, with one hand.

She didn't notice Millie stretch on the hearth-mat and then suddenly rise and dart after her, tail erect as before. As the door opened on to the night Millie sprang forward between her legs.

The girl lurched. She didn't go right down but crashed against the door jamb. There was a brittle bang. The sound was like a knife to the ear—like a brick wrapped in a rag hurled through a shop window—like the breaking of a fine china cup. Like the breaking of a painting on glass.

Louise would have kicked out at Millie but the cat had gone, a black streak into the black night. Not a miaow out there—only a possum grunting and jumping from the skillion verandah roof.

Louise hurried back to the light of the living-room and unwrapped the parcel. And there it lay before her—after three generations—broken cleanly in half. A single break, almost down the middle—a tribute to the quality of the hand-made glass and the wooden backing. Broken . . . after three generations. After the long sailing-ship voyage from China.

Perhaps Chan Ah-Foo had been one of the unlucky Orientals who had not been permitted to land in Victoria because he didn't have the £10 to pay in poll tax, and the ship had carried him on to South Australia. Then Chan Ah-Foo would have carried the painting with loving care in one of the cane baskets suspended on either end of the long bamboo pole across his shoulders, while he followed his countrymen in a long single file across the miles of dry, sparsely inhabited country, stopping sometimes to bury a man not strong enough for such a trek. Now the painting was broken. Louise and Millie had broken it.

She was glad the eyes of the great-grandfather were hidden in the dark of Aunt Eva's bedroom. She hoped that she wouldn't have to hear Aunt Eva say 'It's broke . . .' She tried

43

not to think that the presence of Chan Ah-Foo was in the flickering of the lamp.

Quickly she wrapped the painting again, put it under her arm and went out into the darkness, passing the old lilac heavy with bloom and scent, and around the side of the house and pushed the parcel into the aperture that she knew was there but couldn't see.

Then she went back into the cottage and got into bed. She was still awake, as though she would never go to sleep, when a long time later she heard Eva come home.

CHAPTER SIX

Louise didn't go to sleep until she heard the early roosters crow—the two big fellows with bronze and peacock-blue feathers on Slessors' farm over towards the river—so that she slept heavily for what remained of the night. Mind and body were weary with tossing and she slept late.

She didn't hear Aunt Eva get up, earlier than usual for a Sunday morning, and start up the fire in the stove.

Eva made a cup of tea but she didn't eat anything. She would wait and have breakfast later with Louise. No doubt the girl was tired, waiting up so late for her return. The pile of coals and wood still burning in the fireplace had told her that Louise had sat for a long time by the fire. It made her feel guilty for having left her alone so long, especially after an argument, their first real argument. She even felt guilty for having gone to talk over the matter with Art; it was a kind of disloyalty to Lou.

But Arthur had been helpful. She liked the way he had said, 'The girl knows only the point of view of the young. Only the old can know both points of view, having been young and now being old.'

Eva hadn't thought of herself as being *that* old—as though she should wear the dark colours her mother had said were becoming to the aged—or even that Art himself was *that* old. But she was sure it was a helpful kind of thing to say and so

45

she was tranquil as she sipped the cup of tea, white with milk and heavy with sugar. Arthur had agreed with her that it was time to sell the painting, that now Louise was grown-up the money was needed for extras for the girl. This was one of the results of changed times, of course; with the stores bulging with gear for the kids. Girls hadn't needed so many different kinds of clothes, so much gear, when she was young. In fact, neither clothes, nor the young, had figured in Eva's day.

She recognised that this was a moment of change in their relationship, that nothing would ever be the same between them again . . . between mother and child. No, aunt and child. It was best that she remember this, but she hoped that she had been a mother. Rosemary had not asked her to care for Louise, but Eva had known that her young sister would expect this as a natural outcome—Eva had loved her, and would love and care for her baby. This she had done. She had kept this roof over the child's head—seen that she was warm and fed—and loved her more than anything else in the world. That was why she hadn't married Arty. Sometimes he told her she had been wrong. He had told her again tonight, though he hadn't re-opened his offer.

But he had also said that he would take the painting to the city and sell it for her. He didn't know anything about art himself, except in the lines of a boot or a shoe, or anything at all about such a painting, but he had a niece in the city who had a picture-framing business and who, because art was fashionable, had been business-like enough to learn about painting. She had a modest gallery where young artists and would-bes exhibited. She would know something about Chinese paintings on glass.

'But don't reckon on it being worth much,' he cautioned. Enough perhaps to buy the girl an extra dress or two over the next few years, or until her schooling was finished and she was working herself and could buy her own. 'A bit of glass like that—mightn't be worth anything.' He would take it down to the city next Saturday afternoon, he said, and stay overnight with this niece. The trip wouldn't cost him much that way, and the niece could take the matter from there.

So Eva sipped the hot tea tranquilly and opened Louise's door once to peep at her. The girl's hair was golden on the pillow and her skin smooth. Eva was proud that she had reared her this far, aware that she, herself, had been young to take and rear a child not her own.

She decided then, while the girl slept, to get the painting down ready for Art. Not that she was going to tell Louise what she had in mind, or that she was going to sell it; it would be better if Louise didn't know the source of the extra money. Lou had always been very interested in the story of how they had come by the painting, pestering with questions, and liking the legend Wang Lou had told, even though she giggled at the point where great-grandfather William peeked in at the old Chinese.

Eva, too, had to use the kitchen chair and the stool to reach the top of the wardrobe. When her hands encountered the fluff and dust on the top newspapers, she grimaced. Dust on top of a wardrobe wouldn't suit Julia Burton! Then she grinned to herself. It was the same with all the trades; ten to one a plumber's house would have a leaking spout, and a carpenter a door falling off its hinges.

She lifted down the dusty top layer and screwed it up. It would help light the living-room fire later. Then she felt for the oblong parcel. She felt confidently at first—then urgently. Her fingers didn't believe they couldn't feel it. They quested. Up and down . . . up and down . . . the length of the top tray of the wardrobe, but there was nothing there to feel. Nothing!

She got the two pillows from her bed and put them, one on top of the other, on top of the stool so that she could glimpse over the rail. But there was nothing there. No painting on glass.

She climbed down very slowly and carefully, for the chair and the stool and the pillows made a shaky ladder. She would get Art to look when he called in later. But she knew the painting was gone. It was just not there.

And she knew it was nowhere else in the house.

Her own mother, as a brand-new wife, had been the first to consign the painting to the top of the wardrobe despite the fact that it had already hung above the mantel-piece in the living-room for nigh on forty years. It was the image of great-grandfather's sin, she said—thankful she was related to him only by marriage. The other things 'removed for safety', like Canton ginger and Joss sticks had, of course, long since been eaten or burnt for fun and smelling.

Now the painting was gone.

Someone had stolen it. But who? A few people in the town knew she had it. Especially those who were old enough to remember her mother and recall her taking it down from above the living-room mantel-piece and putting it up on the wardrobe.

Lately, in fact for the last few years, the town had been combed for relics of the golden past. People came up from the city to scrounge the dumps, and the old houses if they could get into them. But Eva had always resisted this, knowing for one thing that she had nothing of value, and being too shy, for another, to think she might have. In any case everything in the cottage was well worn because it had been there so long. Times had never been good enough for her own labouring father to move from the cottage or replace the furnishings. But no doubt one of these antique-hunters had heard about the painting, and wanted it badly enough—and cheaply enough— to steal it.

She would always remember to lock her doors after this.

She put the pillows back on her bed, the wooden stool under the living-room table, and the chair back in the kitchen.

She felt as though she were walking on a road with a shifting bottom. Perhaps quicksands were like this. Certainly the river bottom where the creek flowed into it and rushes grew out from the bank, shifted under your feet, but not sandy, just an ooze of shifting grey mud. She remembered it because, as a child, she had sometimes gone there with Rosemary who had taught herself to swim. Eva had waded into the summer river up to her armpits, hating the squelch of it because Rosemary loved the water and she had felt she should stay close to the younger girl.

As she walked back to the kitchen the irregularities in the floor wavered under her feet.

Yet, ten minutes ago, drinking her tea, she had felt so good.

48

Arthur had said that maybe in two weeks' time—not next week because he wasn't able to go until Saturday, boot-repairing having picked up a little and also because art deals had to be negotiated—the money would come to buy Louise a new dress. Unfortunately, this would not be in time for the school dance. But certainly when the money came there would be no reason then for Lou to go to the city. Eva knew the girl would never come back if she went to the city.

Now it wouldn't be like that. She wouldn't be able to buy the dress for her. Standing in the kitchen, close to the warmth of the stove, she realised how much she had relied on the possession of that painting. That valuable painting. Because of course she knew beyond doubt now that it was valuable. A thief didn't steal a painting unless it was valuable. Very valuable. She trembled at her loss, and felt sick. Right here in this house she had had something that was worth a lot of money, and a thief had taken it.

She knew now that the painting had been to her like a bank account. She had never admitted it even to herself, but that's what the painting had been—a bank account. The thing that would help her to keep Louise when this moment of grown-upness came. Now it wasn't there.

The roof, of course, was still there—but that was leaking.

Arthur would probably want her to go to the police, being a great one for law and order. She hoped he wouldn't persuade her. After all, could you complain about the theft of a thing that you had come by through theft? Not that she ever associated theft with great-grandfather William, despite her mother banishing the Seven Sisters to the top of the wardrobe. He had indeed only removed the painting for its own safety and in the interests of those Chinese relatives in Canton.

But she knew that Arthur believed that the police should do their job, and would say that this was a job for them. He hadn't been able to persuade her to marry him, when he had asked her all those years ago, but there were some things he could persuade her into—like doing the right thing about law and order.

Eva went out then and woke Louise and told her she was

about to cook breakfast. Her stomach still trembled and she didn't think she would be able to eat any breakfast, but she was glad she had never said anything to Louise about her plans for the painting.

CHAPTER SEVEN

Johnathan Baird had said he would come early on the Sunday morning to see what could be done about the apple tree. In this matter, Louise knew that the concern was for the apple tree, not for her. Apple trees were real and important to Johnathan. This one was a late-flowerer. She herself had watched it through the cycle of leaf, sugar-pink bud and white five-petalled flower, and now the embryo apples jostled in clusters on thin stalks just as the flowers had jostled.

She and Aunt Eva had eaten breakfast together and Eva had talked as though yesterday had never been and she had never gone out and left her alone in the cottage and come home late; never even hinted that now she thought Lou was grown up.

Louise had been glad to go along with this make-believe.

Her mind was disturbed and muddled with the breaking of the picture, knowing that nothing could ever make it whole again. Nothing could ever restore it, as it was, to the newspaper nest on top of her aunt's wardrobe. She had broken it. The painting, and Eva telling its story, was part of her own background, of her own growing-up, even though it was funny to think of Chan Ah-Foo, a hundred years ago, sitting huddled up in his bunk beside his dead opium pipe, and great-grandfather peeking in, and deciding to carry away his effects.

But there was nothing funny about breaking something beautiful . . . and valuable. Because now she thought it might be valuable, more valuable than the train fare and board she had

51

been prepared to trade it for. And she didn't know what to do—how to tell Aunt Eva. How to tell Aunt Eva that she had been willing to steal to go to the city. Besides, if she confessed now she would never get to the city. So she was glad to pretend that everything was normal, even though she couldn't meet her aunt's eye.

She told Eva that Johnathan Baird was coming to hoist up the tree.

'Don't let him get rough with it,' Eva said; 'it was there before you and me,'

'He knows about apple trees,' Louise said; 'he's going to be an orchardist.'

Then she heard Johnathan arrive. It was a noisy arrival at the back gate with children shouting and clattering. When she went out she saw that Johnathan was there with his young sister and two brothers. The girl was five years younger than Johnathan, but the two boys had followed her rapidly, with only about a year between each of them. A bad arrangement for Johnathan, Louise thought shrewdly, as such an age gap made him responsible for them. But it seemed that they were with him today for the opposite reason.

As he put his father's wheel-jack on the ground, he said 'Mum didn't believe me when I told her the scratches were from a fall. Not that she said so—just tacked the kids on to me when I was leaving this morning. Gave us a packet of grub and told me to take 'em for a picnic. I tried to leave them home—said I was coming here—but no good. Can't move Mum when she makes up her mind.'

'The picnic sounds all right,' Louise said.

'Would you like to come?'

Louise grinned back. 'I certainly would.'

'Then let's fix this tree, and go.'

Beth and Michael and Andrew stayed out on the paddock, shouting, throwing clods of earth, the boys zinging quartz pebbles at their sister's legs, teasing each other, playing games that were already stupid and silly to Louise because the memory of being as young as they were was still close to her, and shook her when she remembered that in a few weeks she was going to take herself to the city. She noticed, with disapproval, that the two boys had ferrets in a cage.

Johnathan scraped the rich weedy earth from beneath the horizontal trunk, rich here because it had been accepting decades of fallen leaves and apples, and the nutriment from the rubbish heap nearby. He made a hole and placed the jack in it and ordered Louise to find a couple of logs of wood and a brick or two for the bottom.

He smelled this enriched earth—so different from the paddock—while she scrounged the wood and the bricks. 'It'd grow anything,' he said appreciatively, then gave his orders. 'Build the wood on the bricks—shove 'em under as I get the trunk higher.'

He was concerned for the tree and didn't hurry the operation, working two or three feet along the trunk, in case the pressure should cause it to snap.

'If it got down low enough, it'd probably root again,' he said.

Louise crawled in under the tree and the spiky ends of the myriad shoots on the unpruned branches pulled at her hair and caught the threads that were as fine as the spiderwebs she broke as she moved among the branches.

'Been here eighty years, Eva says,' she told him.

'Then it has a long time to go yet,' said the boy. 'Some apple trees can live for two hundred years—far longer than men. Yet they start to bear fruit at four or five and are mature at fifteen.'

He took off his woollen jumper while he worked and she noticed the well-developed muscles in his arms. She thought he looked as strong as the tree.

He worked the jack-lever from the hole he had made and slowly, a fraction at a time, the trunk was levered upwards. When they had finished it was raised only a few inches—the tree being strong and unwilling to yield to change even to save its life.

'That'll do,' Johnathan said, 'mustn't force it too far. The bricks'll stop it from leaning further. Now we can go.'

53

'I'll get some lunch,' Louise said.

'We'll have enough for you. Mum always puts in twice as much as we need.'

But Louise went inside and asked Eva if she might go with Johnathan, as she would have done yesterday, and was given a bag of oatmeal and golden syrup biscuits to take with her.

Johnathan had no fishing-line today and when they started off he led in the opposite direction from that which he had taken yesterday. Pelican Flat evidently had no interest for him today or else, Louise suspected, he was not going to share that interest with her. She was disappointed.

Through the night—listening over and over to the break of glass—she had thought sometimes of Johnathan. The only warm thoughts in a cold clutter. Johnathan would tell her what to do—he would think about this disaster as he had promised to think about her intention to leave the town. She had even thought—when she turned for a moment from her troubles— of what it would be like to go with him to the pictures, if he asked her. But evidently he hadn't drawn as close to her yesterday as she had imagined seeing that he wasn't going to share his problems.

And even with her own worries, she badly wanted to know why Bruce had bashed him—except, of course, that he was not aware that she knew it was Bruce—and why he had gone fishing where there were only mullock heaps.

As they left Ginger Gully behind and set off over the paddock that quickly curled into one rise after another until it finished at a low line of hills, all patterned with stands of ironbark and the occasional redgum, Johnathan said, 'We'll head for the old quartz ovens. Good rabbit country—or used to be—and, anyway, the kids can do a bit of climbing.'

'Would you go there if they weren't with you?'

'No. Mum's shrewd, y'see. Ruined my day for me, of course.'

'Would you have asked me to go if you hadn't had them with you?'

'No.'

He was honest.

The kids were running back and forth, sometimes dawdling

behind to listen to the conversation, especially Beth, who had picked a dandelion and was pulling its seeds apart and tossing them into the air, one by one, as she listened, with seemingly far-away eyes and ears, to every word. Beth irritated Louise; she was only ten but there was an inscrutibility about those hazel eyes as though the girl saw far beyond the limits of her physical eyesight. Louise could imagine Beth knowing that she had broken the Chinese painting; and was especially irritated when she saw Johnathan's devotion to his kid sister. He would break off a sentence to answer a question from her, and stop, himself, to take a pebble out of her shoe when she complained. Yuk . . . thought Louise crossly.

'I'll walk on your heels!' she threatened as the girl dawdled directly in front of her.

'You wouldn't!' scoffed Beth.

'Wouldn't I!' Louise lunged a step forward only missing the girl because Beth moved as quickly.

'You can't!' squealed Beth. 'You don't know how!'

'Try me again!' Louise was purposeful, but the teasing girl went forward to join the other two boys and Louise knew she hadn't made a friend of Beth. Not that it mattered. A rum kind of kid.

As they walked it seemed to Louise that she was not going to be allowed to forget the Chinese painting, for their way took them past the Chinese burial ground. It lay far out of the town, alone, encircled by a rotted post-and-rail fence, over which straggly mess-mate dropped its narrow leaves and tiny stalked seed cups all the year round.

The cemetery was one of the few reminders of the mild pig-tailed men who, for a longer thicker pig-tail, re-inforced their own black hair with horse-hair, drawn from the animal's mane or tail.

Patiently, these small methodical men had 'paddocked' the ground from which the European diggers had already extracted the easier riches. Some had been successful, sending their gold back to China by legal or illegal means, finally returning themselves to live like Mandarins in Canton, or Hong Kong, or some other Chinese province. Some were coolies sent out with overseers from China by wealthy Chinese employers to win gold for them, and were not free to dig for themselves until they had earned their freedom. Some were murdered by resentful Europeans who saw a threat to European workmen in their cheap coolie labour and their low standard of coolie living. Some had turned from gold to market-gardening and life-long labour in an alien land. Some had died in *Hsin-chin-shan*, penniless.

All had brought with them, and retained, their Chinese ways; their industry, their style of food, their opium-smoking and gambling, their building of Joss Houses in which to pay reverence to any one of the number of Chinese war-lords who had benefited China, such as Kwan Kung. Around their Joss Houses they had planted trees of the blue plum—the Honey Prune—and preserved the plums in syrup and given jars of the fruit to the diggers' children at Christmas-time, thereby honouring the Christians' great festival.

Of the Chinese who died on the goldfields those who could afford to cover this contingency did so by pre-arranging for their bodies to be taken back to China for burial. It meant a great deal to a Chinese man to be buried with his ancestors in his own country.

For those who could not afford this last return, ceremonial rites were held about the grave before burial. A whole roast pig and chickens were eaten, and white or rice wine drunk by the mourners, while choice pieces of the meat were left handy at the graveside for the dead to appease his hunger as he entered into the region of the spirits. There was gong-ringing and fireworks and many coloured Joss sticks and papers were burned in the Chinese oven that still stood in the centre of the burial ground.

The oven was an elongated hexagon-shaped pillar, in two sections. The bottom section was the fire-box with an opening for inserting the fuel, and the top section, of similar shape, also had an opening to receive and burn the Joss papers. On top of the structure were four round flat pieces of granite, like pancakes of graduated size, forming a minaret kind of dome.

As Louise walked with the Baird children through this quiet

spot, she had a sudden desire to get close to the oriental man whose painting she had broken. While the two boys fought to be first to climb the oven to sit, like Buddha, on the top round stone, she began to search among the few remaining headstones for one that might bear the name of Chan Ah-Foo.

But she couldn't read any of the names, and so she couldn't discover whether Chan Ah-Foo had prepaid his coffin's passage back to China or whether he lay here, under Australian gum-trees. She ran from one small slab of lichen-encrusted granite to another and then was struck with the thought that perhaps Chan Ah-Foo hadn't been able even to afford to pre-pay for a tombstone. Perhaps he lay under one of the nameless oblong mounds.

But then he had had the painting . . .

Or had great-grandfather William removed it before it could be numbered with his effects?

'Oh, no!' she said aloud, appalled at the idea that great-grandfather's covetousness may have denied the old Chinese a decent burial—which with coffin and feast cost about £8 in those days—or even his body's return to China! And all to no purpose—because the painting had lived most of its life since wrapped in newspaper—and now she had broken it!

'Talks to herself!' taunted Beth.

But Louise paid no heed. A spring sun was shining through the mess-mate, soft sunshine that sprinkled the quiet air with the confetti of leaf-shadow. Yet she shivered a little. She had indeed come close to Chan Ah-Foo . . . wherever he lay . . . here under the gum-trees or as far away as Ning Yi Chien Ho Tien, Kwantung, a northern China province.

'Come on,' grumbled Michael, having barked his knee as he scrambled down from the top of the oven. 'We're going rabbiting. Come on!'

Louise stood still.

'Come on!' echoed Andrew, and shouted to his eldest brother, 'What did'ye have to bring her for?'

He didn't wait for an answer, but ran after Michael who had already jumped the fence, with Beth close behind.

Louise followed them but before climbing over the rotted

fence she looked back and that was when she saw the Chinese man she had noticed in the town yesterday. He was coming through the rusted iron gate on the other side of the graveyard, still wearing his gloves and his neat peaked cap.

Johnathan saw him, too. 'Chinese . . .' he said softly.

'He's probably come to look for an ancestor's grave,' Louise said, voice a little muffled because she found coincidence—strange and exciting coincidence—in the fact that she, herself, had just been searching for a particular name.

'He won't find much here,' Johnathan said practically; 'the Chinese writing has mostly weathered away.'

Louise turned several times to look back, until the mess-mate quite obscured the view, but she saw that the Chinese man was moving slowly and with great respect from one headstone to the next.

CHAPTER EIGHT

Louise would have liked very much to be in Johnathan's confidence, but because she didn't want him to demand *her* confidence and query her interest in things Chinese, she turned away from the subject. Instead, with Beth still ahead, she broached a matter she had been considering all morning, a matter to be brought forward only with Beth out of earshot.

'Are you going to the school dance on Friday, Johnathan?'

'I expect so.' He sounded as though it was not a matter of great import. 'I'm always ready to try anything once.'

'You're taking a girl . . .?' This was hard to ask, like prying.

'No.'

'Then would you . . . be my partner?'

He looked surprised.

'You don't have to . . . unless you want to,' she added hastily.

'Oh . . . that's all right,' said he graciously; 'I'd like to.'

With such an answer she didn't dare ask if he could dance.

Now he asked her a question. 'You haven't changed your mind about going to the city?'

Louise was grateful that he asked this question while Beth couldn't hear, and glad he was aware of this side of his young sister. He was direct, too, when he had something to say. 'No,' she answered. He must surely realise that she couldn't change her mind; that Sheila's cast-off dress was a label she was not prepared to wear.

'I think you should. I don't know how you can even think of going to live in the city. Wouldn't suit me.'

'We can't all be the same,' she said fiercely.

'No-o . . . I suppose not. Have you thought any more about money?'

'Yes.' She had thought all night about money, about the broken painting.

'Where are you going to get it?'

'I don't know.' If he had asked the direct question yesterday she would probably have made some evasive reply or, if he had persisted, told him about the painting. Through the night she had actually visualised herself seeking his advice for what she should do now that the painting was broken, but today somehow she couldn't tell him what she had done to Chan Ah-Foo's painting.

'I reckon I've got enough for my train fare down,' she said. 'I'll just have to hope I get a job right away.'

'Where'll you sleep and where'll you eat in the meantime?'

'Something'll turn up.'

'If you don't get somewhere to board, you might get picked up for vagrancy,' he said it very calmly, having read in the Saturday's newspaper about a girl charged with vagrancy.

'I wouldn't!' Louise flashed. 'I don't look—I'm not!—that sort. Some boarding-house will take me. They could phone the place where I get a job for proof that I'll be able to pay at the end of the week.'

'*If* you get a job. Even Uni students have trouble getting jobs. And quite often the pay isn't enough to cover board.'

Louise ignored the last remark. 'Of course I'll get a job. I'm not dumb—I'm quick at figures; and I reckon I could sell things in a shop. I did pretty well at the school bazaar last term—sold more than anyone else. And if it's a factory well . . . repetition work is easy enough.'

'What about your mum?'

'I told you—she's not my mother. She's my aunt. She just got stuck with me. Anyone could've got me.'

'Still don't reckon you should,' said Johnathan.

He wished she would just forget about all this; just stay with her aunt, wear the red dress—it suited her very well—and not create problems. He didn't really want her problem—he had

60

his own—but he couldn't see her stuck. They'd got themselves involved together over that bashing, and he was grateful for what she had done.

'I can lend you a few dollars,' he said, with some caution. It wouldn't be wise to tell her too much. But she was quite pretty, with nice hair and her lips had nice curves and were red; she sort of made him feel . . . well . . . that he was a man. To be able to lend her money . . . this was the province of the male.

'Johnathan!' her eyes brightened at once. She felt secure and cared-for and safe with Johnathan offering to lend her the money. Now she could go without any trouble or fears, without even having to carry the painting to Melbourne and hawk it perhaps from dealer to dealer. Except that there wasn't a painting now to hawk. 'Thank you!' she cried. 'I'll only need to borrow it for a week or two—just till I get set up.'

Her shining eyes almost repaid Johnathan for what he was offering.

'I'll go the week-end after next,' she said.

'Week-end after next! That's not going to give me much time to get some money together.' He didn't tell her he had a bank account because, obviously, he couldn't use bank money to help her. For one thing, if anyone happened to see his pass-book they might ask why he had withdrawn the money. This would not only betray Louise but certainly embarrass himself.

Louise protested. 'But you just said about the Uni students going after jobs—so I feel the sooner I get down there the better chance I'll have.'

'I suppose you're right,' he said grudgingly, frowning. She was going to be a responsibility—and he was aware of some discomfort. 'I'll do what I can.'

'Oh, Johnathan thank you!' She spoke so loudly and with such enthusiasm that Beth looked round and said to Michael and Andrew in a way that humiliated her, 'I thought she was going to kiss him!'

Neither Johnathan nor Louise spoke for a long time after that; not until they topped a fold in the hills where, in the hollow, the crumbling brickwork of the quartz kilns on the old battery site were all that remained of the Rabbit's Paw lode mine. On one side was a great slag heap and on the other the rusted remnants of the old winding and pumping engines. The Rabbit's Paw had yielded many thousands of ounces of gold before it closed down at the turn of the century. For safety the shaft had been sealed off, and only some of the timbering, enormous splintered wooden beams studded with giant rusty bolts, remained on the surface. Peppercorn trees overhung the shallow basin that had been the mouth of the shaft, and extended over the kilns. Scattered around were fragments of slate and quartz and gravel.

The young Bairds liked to come here. There was always the chance of a rabbit, and they also liked to climb into the cup-shaped ovens in which ten tons of rock at a time had been roasted by the five tons of firewood smouldering underneath, thereby decomposing the pyrites and drawing off such impurities as sulphur and arsenic. Johnathan, too, had his own reasons for selecting this picnic spot, Louise felt.

'Do you always use ferrets?' She forced herself to break the embarrassment.

'Yeah. The kids like them. And Mum is always glad of a rabbit—a bit of free meat. Used to be plenty of 'em around here. But they've thinned out, and you have to watch that you don't get on to myxos.'

'I don't like ferrets,' she said.

Now they were on the hill-side itself which was riddled with burrows like a pepper-pot.

'Mostly old holes,' said Johnathan.

Louise could see that. Some of the burrows were so stale that sandflies buzzed about the entrance.

'Then why did you bring the kids rabbiting here?' she asked, surprised.

But Johnathan had turned away and didn't answer.

The two younger Baird boys, with only a year between them, were much alike. They were red-headed, freckled and treated Louise as though she wasn't there yet at the same time managed to make her feel like an insect under a microscope and—because of her—were off-hand and cheeky with Johnathan, and Beth, too. They were a segment in themselves.

Andrew selected a rabbit-burrow and Michael uncaged the first ferret. It was a rich creamy colour, with black spots on its tiny feet. It had a long snout for burrowing and a long body.

'It's got very small bones,' Johnathan said, 'and when it wants to go through a narrow space it expels air out of that big abdomen—squeezes itself up to nothing. You can train a ferret to know its master and take it walking on a lead like a dog.'

'I don't like ferrets,' said Louise again, 'something mean about them—going into another animal's home and hunting it out to be killed.'

'We're glad of the rabbits for tucker,' Johnathan said again, 'costs a lot to keep our family. A ferret's pretty when he runs— bunches up his stomach, holds his tail up straight, and patters along on those tiny feet. Looks a bit like a squirrel.'

'That one is not friendly,' said Louise, as the sinuous sharp-toothed animal snapped at Michael.

'He's hungry. Have to keep them a bit hungry when you're going after rabbits.'

'I thought you loved the country . . . and that's the animals, too, isn't it?'

'Even a farmer has to be practical,' said Johnathan patiently. This girl seemed to see-saw on her thoughts; he found it hard to keep pace with her.

Louise turned away. The red-headed boys were kept busy with their ferrets but they didn't catch a rabbit, and Louise was glad.

Lunch was a noisy time. Michael and Andrew ran about aimlessly, kicking at stones, scuffling, climbing a scraggy wattle, then both making a wattle switch and chasing each other. Nor did they forget to take swipes at the calves of Beth's legs in between times, until they stung her into crying and Johnathan threatened that they would not get any cake.

After lunch Johnathan said to Louise, 'Listen, I've got a message to deliver for Mum to old Quin—you know the old bloke who lives the other side of this hill?'

Yes, she knew old Quin, the ancient prospector, who came

in from the bush every Saturday morning to buy his provisions. Everyone knew old Quin, even if he didn't know you and you'd never spoken to him. He had a three-legged dog that always waited outside the various stores, shivering whether the day was hot or cold, while the old man did his shopping. Quin had found the dog, injured, on the road; evidently it had been swept off the open tray of a truck swaying on the sharp corner. He'd paid the vet a lot of money to fix the dog.

'I'll nip over there now—you can stay and watch the kids. See none of them get stuck in a burrow,' Johnathan said.

He was gone before she could protest, and she knew he went quickly so that she wouldn't ask to go with him. The two boys seemed surprised to see him disappear over the hill, but not Beth. Without doubt Beth shared her brother's life. But somehow Louise didn't believe about the message for Quin. The way Johnathan took off, almost guiltily, caused her to doubt. On the other hand . . . did he find the Ovens a good picnic place because it was not too far from Quin's?

'Are your father and mother friendly with the old man?' she asked Beth.

The child answered very pleasantly. 'Of course. He's Mum's cousin, or something.'

'Does Johnathan often have to take messages to him?'

'Of course.'

Louise looked at the hazel eyes with their long lashes. She had never seen such long *real* lashes on anyone. Sheila had had some false ones but they hadn't looked as good as Beth's real ones.

'I'm going up the hill to the boys,' Beth said, which really meant that she didn't want to be asked any more questions and made Louise even more certain that Beth knew where Johnathan had gone, whether it was to Quin's or somewhere else.

This hill was the tallest of the folded hills, rising above the kilns, with boulders on it and gorse and Chinese coffee bush and wattle straggling. It was pock-marked with old burrows as though the remnants of all the colonies of rabbits that had once overrun the gullies and the mines—causing many a cave-in after the miners left—had gathered here. But myxomatosis had wiped out vast numbers of them.

The boys didn't seem to be having much luck with their ferrets but now, as Beth set off to join them, there was a sudden shout as a rabbit shot out, escaping the net because a root snagged the draw-string. The two boys were near the top of the hill and they both jumped and sprang after the rabbit to note its direction. They scurried dirt and stones down the hill and then, just when Beth was halfway, they disturbed a large boulder. It teetered, swayed and began to roll . . . slowly at first . . . like a clumsy fat man trying to dance.

Beth and Louise both looked up at the same time—Beth from halfway up the hill and Louise from the bottom.

The boulder rolled quite slowly at first, as if surprised to find itself on the move after balancing so long. Perhaps it had balanced a million years—perhaps ten million.

It was the kernel of a once greater rock, maybe a knoll itself once, whose softer outer covering had been eroded from around it, leaving it naked. And naked it had been beaten by the rain and ravaged by the wind and burned by the sun until it had shrunk to just a large boulder that could be disturbed by an excited boy giving it an accidental push.

It rolled faster.

'Beth!' cried Louise.

From the bottom of the hill Louise saw that the boulder must look monstrous to a small girl looking upwards . . . watching it bump down towards her. Faster now . . . tearing out the gorse and the Chinese coffee bush, splintering the young wattle, crushing to fragments the bits of slate and quartz . . . bumping down . . . heavy, grotesque . . . a fat body without legs.

Not coming straight but feinting and dodging as though pursued. Yet nothing pursued the legless monster. Nothing directed its path but the vagary of the uneven ground . . . thrusting it this way . . . pushing it that way . . . tumbling it on to its side . . . on to its belly . . . on to its faceless face.

The child did not move but stared upwards.

'Look out!' cried Louise.

Beth turned her head slightly.

'Look out! Watch it! Don't jump yet. Wait until you see which way it's going. Wait . . . until it's near enough to see-e!' Her voice was caught up by the wind and tossed over the hill.

She prayed her advice was right . . . that when Beth jumped she would have seen which way to jump. Otherwise her fate would be the same as the Chinese coffee bush, the young wattle, the fragmented slate and quartz.

The boulder was coming fast now. The noise of it was the thumping of rock on rock, and dust rising and small stones flinging and spitting. Louise strained to follow its course . . . strained to see the contour of the land underneath the dress of kangaroo grass.

'Now!' she cried. 'Now . . . towards that gorse! Jump!'

The girl hesitated.

'Jump!' Louise shrieked. 'Towards the gorse! The *gorse-e!*'

Beth jumped and the boulder hurtled over the spot where she had stood and kept coming faster . . . and faster . . . and faster . . . a great mindless body of rock seeking a safe resting-place and stopping at last in the hollow in the bottom. There was dust in the air, and the reverberations of its passing on the hill, and the boys racing after it. Two red-headed boys with their ferrets and rabbits forgotten.

'Are you all right! Beth!'

They raced at Beth and clutched at her halfway down the hillside, clung to her, shook her to see that she still worked.

'Are you all right!' The whiteness of their faces made their hair redder still.

'Yes . . . yes!' Beth breathed, her nostrils wide open as though she couldn't get enough air.

'Thought you was a goner!' cried Michael.

'Me, too,' said Andrew.

Both let go their clutching grip so suddenly that the girl swayed. But they had revealed that she was important to them.

'I only had to jump . . .' she said, so that they wouldn't feel so badly about it, and rather enjoying being important.

'What'll Mum say!' relished Michael.

'You mustn't tell her!' said Beth at once. 'Because then she'll want to know where Johnathan was. You mustn't tell her.'

'He went to Quin's,' said Andrew.

'Yes—but he should have taken the message on our way out this morning. We mustn't tell her.'

Louise was certain then that Johnathan hadn't had a message for Quin, because he couldn't have delivered the message on the way out. Quin's place was over the hill, further on.

The boys were relieved not to have to tell, seeing they had started the stone rolling, and as Beth was not hurt they went back to their ferrets and their rabbit burrows.

Louise was jealous that Beth was in her brother's confidence and knew his real activities for the afternoon. She felt that she should have known, too. She had told him her troubles, or some of them.

Nevertheless, as they walked home, she was content. It wouldn't take long to pay back to Johnathan the money he was going to lend her. And she would pay her aunt for the picture, too. That would take longer but she would find out what it had been worth, unbroken, and pay her aunt. No doubt she would be able to do this before Eva found out that it had even left its nest of paper. It was only a couple of months or so since Eva had renewed the paper and was not likely to change it again before spring of next year. There was plenty of time. Louise thought her aunt would be pleased when she gave her the money.

To reach home there was no need for the Bairds to go past the miner's cottage so Louise said goodbye before the cottage came into view. But when she was still some distance from the house she was startled to see the local policeman come out the front door, adjust his crash-helmet and turn his police-bike towards the road.

CHAPTER NINE

Louise started to run, but though the policeman walked his bike back to the gravel road, he had disappeared in the direction of the town by the time she reached the gate.

She opened the front door that led directly into the living-room and that had just enough swing-space to clear Aunt Eva's chair as she sat by the fire.

Eva was doing a bit of knitting. She knitted always with thick-ply wool, in serviceable colours, and made clumsy-looking cardigans and jumpers for herself and Louise. Sometimes she made a jumper for Art, but only when his last one was dropping into holes. Louise didn't mind the heavy-looking garments, and Sheila said they were trendy.

Her aunt didn't look as though she had just had a visit from the local policeman, the first Louise could ever remember. Nor did she volunteer to tell Louise why.

Louise had to ask. 'I saw Hennessy go . . . the cop . . .?'

'Oh . . . did you . . ?' Obviously, Eva had hoped Lou hadn't seen Hennessy.

'Why did he come here?'

'Well-l . . . Art sent him.'

'Why?'

With Louise staring at her, Eva couldn't escape answering. 'The painting—that Chinese painting—seems to have disappeared from the top of my wardrobe.'

'The Chinese painting!' Louise's surprise was genuine. She

68

just hadn't connected the policeman's visit with the painting. It hadn't occurred to her that Eva would already have discovered its removal.

'Art said I had to report that it had been stolen—you have to be on the side of law and order, he said. Too many people think they can do anything they like these days, he said. He reckons I'm lucky someone didn't bash me for it.'

'Stolen . . .' said Louise, not very loudly.

'Yes. He says people'll do anything for money these days. Some of these fellows that come up from the city looking for the old things. He says someone must have heard of it, and reckoned it was valuable.'

'Oh . . .'

'But I don't want you to worry about it, Lou. I wasn't going to tell you. No use both of us being upset. It's gone and that's that. Hennessy's going to put a notice on the police-station door, asking anyone who saw a person carrying a parcel wrapped in newspaper that could have been a painting—or seeing one in a car—to report the matter at once. And tomorrow there'll be a description of it in the paper. He asked me to describe it. He was very interested in the bit about the Seven Sisters—like Wang Lou told me.'

Eva knitted stolidly. She was never going to let Louise know how her hopes had centred around that painting. Although now that she knew it was valuable enough for someone to steal her disappointment hurt inside like a pain. But she couldn't bring herself to tell Louise what she had hoped from the painting.

And Louise thought: 'I can't tell her that I took it—and broke it. Not now. The story would go right through the town. It would be like walking around naked. Eva would want to know—people would want to know—why I took it. That would bring us back to the red dress.' There were whys and wherefores that you couldn't throw down to the public. It would reveal too clearly the no-accountness of their lives.

'Are you very upset?' she forced herself to ask.

'No,' lied Eva; 'in any case, Hennessy thinks we'll get it back. It's a hard thing to dispose of, he said—and Art said so, too. The thief will have to wait awhile before he tries to sell it—unless he's already got his buyer lined up. All I hope is—it breaks on him!' Eva was bitter.

'Maybe it will,' said Louise; 'it's only glass. Glass can break.'

And there the matter ended, for Eva did not want to talk about it, and neither did Louise. But as Eva did not buy a morning paper except on Saturday, Louise read an account of the robbery in the next day's local newspaper, which was always available in the school library. The painting was described in some detail, and Louise realised then that Eva had looked at it many times, with admiring and possessive eyes. It had evidently meant much more to her than the story told of a great-grandfather.

Eva worked at the Burtons' house on Mondays, spending a long full day cleaning and ironing which meant that Louise always arrived home ahead of her.

Today she hurried from school, and went first to the side of the house under which she had hidden the painting. Although there was no neighbouring house on this side of the cottage, she made sure there was no one in sight before she went down the slate path between the overgrown flower beds where fuchsias and a lilac were as tall as trees, and white daisy grew rank. She took another quick look across deserted Ginger Gully before she knelt down and stretched her arm and pushed the cracked painting as far under the low floor boards as she could. Then she brought a few broken bricks and placed them strategically, but with deceptive casualness in the opening and heaped the garden leaves and rubbish up around them.

The painting would remain there now, she thought, with some sadness, until the house itself fell in on it.

The sadness continued for the rest of the week, nevertheless she and Eva were quite comfortable together.

Then came Friday, and the school dance.

Johnathan called for her at eight o'clock. They had not said much to each other during the week; and they talked very little as they walked together now across the dark paddock.

It was a new experience walking with a boy . . . going out

with a boy alone . . . at night. Louise had wondered all the week if Johnathan's father would come with his grey utility and take them to the hall, and even pick them up afterwards. But Johnathan had not suggested this and here they were, walking.

Louise was wearing the pale blue summer dress she had worn to the school dance last year. She could not bring herself to wear the red dress or either of Sheila's two summer dresses and, surprisingly, Eva did not press the point.

She didn't have nail polish or a hair-do as most of the girls would have, as Sheila had had last year. Sheila's hair had been piled high with big sausage curls across the top. Even to Louise she had looked a stranger. But Sheila had had all the dances and Billy Brand, a prefect, would have walked home with her if her father hadn't been picking her up. Sheila had been angry about that. 'As if we're kids!' She complained to Louise the next day, the set combed out of her hair and the nail polish removed. ·

Last year Sheila had shared her nail polish and lipstick and Louise had felt dressed-up enough—because she was younger then, she now supposed. In any case, last year, she hadn't really cared whether or not anyone asked her to dance.

She hadn't been bursting to dance. She thought that the boys looked funny milling around the door—short ones, tall ones; some had short hair, back and sides, and hair oil, others no hair oil and stiff springy hair that was as long as the school principal would allow—all waiting for the young science master to lead on to the floor. It was quite a triumph for Sheila that the young master asked her for the first dance. That set the tempo of the night for Sheila.

Louise had liked the music, had tapped her feet and hadn't minded sitting out most of the dances with the group of girls not in demand. And Sheila always came back and sat beside her. Sheila looked very hot all night and her eyes were as shiny as stars.

But this year's school dance would be different. Sheila would not be there. Louise had no nail polish and Eva could not afford for her to have a hair-do while last year's dress, now facing its second summer, was tight. Added to which this year she would sit beside Johnathan.

But somehow she did not think he would be concerned about what she looked like, or what she wore. He was too interested in apple trees and orchards. Nevertheless, for his sake, she hoped that someone else would ask her to dance. Even a boy like Johnathan might be embarrassed if no one wanted to dance with her; at the same time she was not sure that she wanted that someone to be Bruce.

The annual school dance was held in the old stone Mechanics Institute Hall, which had a bit of gravelled courtyard at the side where vehicles could be parked off the street. But it was chosen mainly because it had only two entrances, a front and a rear, which made it easy for authority to prevent the entry of the uninvited.

Inside everything looked much the same as last year, with swathes and drapes of coloured paper floating from the high ceiling, and balloons hanging in bunches of rainbow grapes, all put up at the risk of necks by the young and acrobatic Dance Committee. The same boys could have been milling around the door; in fact many of them probably were the same boys except that they were a year older, and some were youngsters, first year out of primary school.

Louise led the way across the hall to where the group of unescorted girls congregated; this was intentional, in case Johnathan took fright, or lost interest, and left her unattended. She staked their claim to two of the wooden seats which backed against the walls by draping her cardigan, length-wise over two backs.

In this group her last year's dress didn't stand out; some of these girls, like some of the boys, were just out of primary and not even up to pantyhose; some were older than Louise and wore long dresses, and were self-conscious. They were a group, yet each separate, the giggling, the glum, and even the glamorous.

Bruce, she noted, was one of a party that staked a claim to a corner with the least draught where all the girls were gay, tossing witty words over their shoulders like the chiffon scarf that Diane, Bruce's girl, wore, and all looking grown-up. In fact, when Diane got too hot and discarded the chiffon scarf, Louise was surprised to see that her frock was strapless. Mr Pinkerton, the principal, had warned them. *No* strapless dresses—even for those for whom this would be the last annual school dance. Such dresses only made the very young ones feel like children at a grown-ups' party, Mr Pinkerton said, and they had the right to enjoy their annual dance as much as the school-leavers—even if some of the latter were old enough, and their parents were rich enough, for them to drive in their own cars to school.

Louise was just admiring Diane's tanned shoulders when she saw Mrs Pinkerton—no doubt at the instigation of Mr Pinkerton—who was wide, short and round, present Diane with her own 40-inch-bust grey cardigan to be worn for the rest of the evening! As Mrs Pinkerton kept herself warm in a pink cardigan, it seemed that Mr Pinkerton had prepared for all possibilities.

Bruce, she saw, still had the remnants of a bruise around his eye. He smiled at her across the hall but he didn't ask her to dance; and when he passed, dancing with Diane, she could smell the mingled smells of heavy perfume and after-shave lotion, and registered that she and Johnathan didn't smell of anything. Which surely signified they were very small cheese.

Johnathan trod on her toes as Bruce had predicted, but at least he was willing to attempt to dance whenever it looked as though she wasn't going to get a partner. He told her, as a conversation piece, that his parents had spent a lot of time during the week teaching him in readiness for tonight. But surprisingly Louise had more invitations to get up than she expected and didn't disgrace him by being a wallflower. When she danced with others Johnathan was one of those who milled around the door.

But he always came back as soon as she was seated and, at supper-time, twice fought his way through the bee swarm in the adjacent supper-room where members of the Parents' Committee were serving out food: the first time to secure the hottest of sausage rolls and the creamiest of cakes, and the second for a jug of fruit cup. Louise had wondered how he would shape up to this challenge. Sheila had once lost interest in a boy because he hung back at supper-time.

The band was up on the stage, with microphone and sound boxes placed to give maximum volume. From this stage, too, lights were played on the dancers. Once Johnathan said: 'You've turned purple,' as though she were going to stay that way.

'I look awful?' Louise said quickly.

'Oh, no,' said Johnathan, as though he couldn't bear purple, and looked beyond her to all the other purple dancers.

Once, just after supper, there was a commotion at the front door when some of the uninvited local youth—who roamed at night and threw stones on people's roofs and kept Senior-Constable Hennessy in training for the annual Police Sports—attempted to gate-crash. But Senior-Constable Hennessy came quickly from the supper-room, burning his throat with the swift swallow of the hottest of those hot sausage rolls, and dispersed them. A little later someone, probably the same group, switched off the lights at the outside meter, and there were squeals, some of happy fear, in the sudden blackness.

Louise and Johnathan were dancing together when that happened and when they went back to their seats, they found that Johnathan's coat—his father's best sportscoat—which Johnathan had also hung over the chair, was missing. Louise remembered then that Bruce had been dancing quite near them when the lights went out.

Apparently Johnathan remembered, too, for without a word he left his partner standing and dived for the door, snatched the pass-out check the schoolgirl thrust at him, jumped across the foyer and down the steps into the shadows of the car-park.

Louise followed him, not waiting even to grab up her cardigan. The sudden setting of his mouth had alarmed her. Johnathan was always so mild, so sensible and understanding, his expression as a rule either quiet or merry, but the set of his mouth now made her think of a steel rabbit-trap, shut fast.

She raced down the steps and the darkness raced to meet her and swallowed her up as it had swallowed Johnathan.

Cars were parked haphazardly. Shadows of people moved here and there but they moved too casually, and laughed or giggled, so that she knew they were neither Bruce nor Johnathan.

She went up and down between the cars, aware of the cold and wishing she might call out for Johnathan, but knowing this would not be wise. She didn't want to draw the attention of Mr Pinkerton, or any master's attention, or the attention of the parents who were washing up after supper, or the attention of Senior-Constable Hennessy, or the attention of the strays who might still be skulking beyond the perimeter of the light. Some of these could well be looking for Johnathan, too.

Johnathan was strong and big, but he was a loner. Bruce had a gang.

Louise shivered. Whatever was going on between them was not her business, yet somehow she was involved.

The night wind was cold, touching her body with dry cold fingers as she searched. From inside the hall she could hear the music starting up 'Auld Lang Syne'. She was sorry to miss this part of the evening . . . forming the big circle, holding hands and singing, then crossing arms to draw your neighbour closer and dancing into the centre and out again. It was this moment last year that had made her feel one of the group, not just Louise. It had been a warm feeling to tingle at the human current in the hands, to be part of a large body, not just encased in her own limited shell. She was sorry to miss this moment tonight.

But she had to find Johnathan quickly. There must be no sign of any kind of trouble when the crowd left the hall. It must not get to the notice of Mr Pinkerton, or Senior-Constable Hennessy—at least they must not know that Johnathan was involved. There had been so much trouble last year that the headmaster had said this would be the last annual dance if it occurred again—and the ringleaders would be summarily expelled.

Of one thing Louise was sure—Johnathan's involvement was forced, not voluntary. That was why she had to find him quickly.

She did find him at length—both of them—behind the back

of the hall with the old-fashioned conveniences in either corner of the block and a grassy patch in the middle. They were fighting.

A pale street light from over the rear fence gave enough illumination for her to see that it was them. There were other figures standing back in the shadows thrown by the line of peppercorn trees along the fence, but so far they hadn't joined in. They would wait no doubt until Johnathan was on the ground before closing in.

She moved in as close as she dared, not with any intention of stopping the fight, which she knew she could not do, but so that her light-coloured dress would reveal her presence. Even if they didn't recognise who she was, they would know that someone was witnessing what was happening.

She stood there trembling. The boys were thumping each other, each gasping when a blow knocked out the breath, gulping jerkily to take air in again, arms lashing out and sometimes smashing only the air.

Johnathan was shorter than Bruce but almost as heavy. This was not an unequal contest . . . with one boy on the ground.

Then suddenly there was agitation on the sidelines.

'S'sst—cop's comin'!'

Repeated by each one as he dissolved into shadow. 'S'sst—cop's comin'!'

'S'sst—cop's comin'!'

The fight ceased abruptly. Louise felt her hand grasped and she was jerked into the darkness under the fronds of the peppercorns and then through a gap in the paling fence. She went willingly because she knew it was Johnathan who had her hand. She ran with him across the vacant allotment behind the hall where the town's first hotel, a weatherboard building, had stood until a few months ago. It had been pulled down because the white ants had eaten the stumps. And now no one in the town could think of any good reason to build something in its place. It would be a vacant allotment in the middle of the town for a long time.

She dragged back suddenly. 'My cardigan . . . I left it in the hall!'

'We can't go back!' gasped the boy. 'Old Hennessy'll be waiting still . . . and Pinkerton.'

'I'm cold!'

'Cold! . . . running like this!' Then he snapped. 'Put this on!'

Now she saw that Johnathan was carrying his father's sports coat. That was what he had scooped up from the ground as they fled from behind the hall.

'Might be a bit muddy—that drip dragged it through a puddle as he dodged ahead of me.'

'What'll your father say?'

'It's my mum that'll say. Unless I can brush the dirt off and she doesn't find out. Only I got a whack in the eye myself this time—don't think she'll miss that.'

'But why . . .?'

'I'll tell you sometime. Not now.'

They ran on, down the empty end of the main street where the shops were dark, except for one wary vendor of electrical goods, and not even a milk-bar. When they turned into one of the side streets he eased their pace a little and began to speak again.

'Listen, have you got anything lined up for the week-end— tomorrow and Sunday?'

'No-o.' This wasn't quite true. Last night she had put most of the clothes she intended to take to the city—only a week away now—into Rosemary's old suitcase and hidden it under her bed, planning to do any necessary mending of the articles during the week-end.

'Then will you come out again with me and the kids . . . sort of . . . picnicking . . . like we did last Sunday?'

'Well-l . . . all right.' She couldn't very well refuse if he was going to lend her her fare to the city. But she wondered at once if his invitation was really to placate, or even hoodwink, his mother. Was she being used as a blind?

'O.K.—I'll pick you up same time tomorrow.'

He ceased to run now but walked very quickly, down a couple of lanes paved with slate slabs, past some houses already darkened and finally on to the gravelled road that linked up with the track that led to her front gate. He walked very quickly indeed, apparently eager to get home or rid of her She didn't quite know whether she should be glad or sorry. She had rather dreaded he might want to kiss her good-night, though he had never appeared to her as the kissing sort. But then Sheila, who had had some experience, said that you just never could tell.

But when he pushed her inside the front gate, grabbed the coat off her shoulders and hurried away, she didn't know whether to be relieved or to feel rejected.

CHAPTER TEN

Louise slept a bit late the next morning, but Eva waited to have breakfast with her. Over breakfast Louise told her aunt that she was going on another picnic with Johnathan today, and tomorrow also. As Johnathan hadn't given her any reason for the excursions—and Eva would expect one—she said that Mrs Baird had complained to Johnathan that he was not spending enough time with his young brothers and sister, and this was his way of doing it.

She had half-expected Eva to raise an objection; to say that, as Johnathan was a boy, she was seeing too much of him. But Eva raised no objection. There had been something different about Eva all the week, a kind of nervousness. Louise wondered if this was because she believed a thief had been in the house, and certainly she herself would not like the thought, if such were really the case.

The idea of some strange person—evil because he had come into the house to steal—touching the things they handled, looking at the things that were theirs, being amused because there was so little of value in the home, must be upsetting for Eva. Even though the police had been unable to find finger-prints—which showed that he was a professional and used gloves, Senior-Constable Hennessy said—wouldn't get rid of the feeling that he had touched everything, looked at every-thing, evaluated everything.

Eva locked the doors at night now, and always called out

to Louise to let her know if she were going out into the yard after dark. The loss of the painting had frightened her.

Louise was sorry about this. She wished she could tell her aunt that it was she who had removed the painting. But she couldn't bring herself to do so; she couldn't face what further things the town might say of them. There had already been so much in the newspaper about it—even a picture of their cottage, looking like someone's outhouse. She just couldn't admit to having taken the painting herself. In any case, it was probably kinder now to let Eva think it was stolen than to know it was broken.

Her aunt may have been worried, too, because she had said she was leaving her for the city. Eva looked at her at times as if she wanted to ask if she were still going, but she never did.

They were both drinking a second cup of tea and Louise was making an extra piece of toast at the fire-stove when a car pulled up on the unmade track in the front of the cottage. Louise heard the sound of the car and, from where she stood by the stove, she could see through the connecting door between kitchen and living-room and through the front window.

'It's Mrs Burton!' she told Eva. 'What on earth could she want at this hour on Saturday morning!'

Eva put her cup down noisily. 'Mrs Burton! But she never comes here—at any hour! She's *never* been here.'

Louise was thinking the same and her face reddened, though it may have been that she was standing too close to the stove.

'You let her in, Lou—I'll have to comb my hair!'

Eva's hair was as tidy as it always was or could be, but Louise understood that she had to slip into the bedroom for a moment to gather herself together, to prepare herself to meet her employer in the nakedness of her own home. Louise's lip twitched—why was Eva always so conscious of her own inferiority?

'I'll take off my apron,' Eva said. 'You straighten the table a bit . . . quickly.'

'She won't notice,' Louise said, seeing in her mind's eye Julia Burton's smart kitchen with its modern appliances. Julia would find the cottage kitchen crude, and their manner of having breakfast even more crude. 'She's come for something—not to look at your kitchen.'

Eva disappeared into her bedroom, dodging through the door quickly in case Julia saw her through the window. She felt quite trembly at the idea of Mrs Burton in her kitchen. Perhaps after she saw it her employer would doubt her ability to keep the bank kitchen so shiny, or perhaps she would not give her a reference good enough to impress the incoming banker. The new banker's wife might decide to employ the male cleaners who did so many of the town's houses now, going around in a light van and having their own vacuum cleaners and polishers. With their man's extra strength and reach, they were out of a place in an hour or two, freeing the lady of the house so quickly of their presence. Eva was upset. She couldn't afford to lose a place now. And she could think of no good reason for Julia Burton's visit.

Louise had to answer the quick knock on the door because Eva didn't come out of her bedroom. She went with the toasting-fork still in her hand; after all, she was not to know, was she, that Julia Burton was knocking?

'Louise! I'm so glad you're home.' Julia stepped straight into the cottage. 'I was afraid you might have already gone to the shops . . . being Saturday morning . . . and I didn't want to miss you. That's why I came early.'

'You came to see me?' said Louise, surprised.

'Yes—I'm so worried.'

Louise shut the door with her right hand, the toasting-fork sticking out from her left like a weapon of defence. 'I'll put this thing down.'

'No—finish your toasting. We can talk while you eat.'

Louise felt this wasn't going to be a very enjoyable piece of toast but she went back to the kitchen and Sheila's mother followed her, and by the time Eva appeared had sat down on a hard kitchen chair.

'Mrs Burton . . .' said Eva, relieved that the visit was not for her, yet no less perturbed that it was for Louise.

'Eva—I had to come. To talk to Louise. I thought she might be able to tell me something of what happened last night.'

81

Louise's back was to the two women while she finished toasting the piece of bread. So that was it. She should have guessed.

'Was Bruce at the dance last night, Louise?'

'Yes.'

'What happened?'

'What do you mean, Mrs Burton?'

'Who hit him?'

Louise had to think carefully, had to have time to think, so she took a large lump of butter on her knife and spread it on the slice of toast very slowly, and didn't look at Bruce's mother.

'He came home with a cut on the lip that needed a stitch . . . and his clothes a mess.'

'Lou . . . you didn't say anything about it!' cried Eva.

'I smiled at Bruce a couple of times across the hall during the evening,' Louise spoke slowly 'I didn't dance with him, or actually speak with him once.'

'But you must have seen something . . . or heard something,' Julia demanded. 'I have to know, Louise—there are going to be questions asked when he goes to school on Monday. He's already in a precarious position there. Another false step and he's out. And where to—if that happens?'

'You must have seen something, Lou,' said Eva, desperate for Louise to do the right thing by her employer.

'There was the usual pack outside the hall,' the girl said, hoping this was not giving too much away; 'and the lights were put out once. But from inside you couldn't hear what was going on outside. I can't help you, Mrs Burton.'

'Bruce says it was a boy named Johnathan Baird,' said Julia Burton; 'son of the man who's recently taken over that Corner Store. He says Johnathan waylaid him after the dance and sprang at him out of the dark.'

'Johnathan!' gasped Eva, staring at Louise.

'What else did Bruce say?' asked Louise, very coldly.

'Well-l . . . that's about all. At least, all that I could get out of him, except that the attack was quite unprovoked.'

'Lou . . .?' Eva was looking at her, expecting her to tell Mrs

82

Burton the facts that she felt Mrs Burton should know and which Louise, obviously, must already know.

But Louise was trying to think how this was going to affect Johnathan. The only thing she knew about the situation was that it was Johnathan who had been provoked—his father's sports coat taken from the hall and dragged through the mud. And last week being kicked by the gang as he lay on the ground. She didn't know what the trouble was between them.

She kept on buttering her toast and spreading it with mulberry jam which she didn't like. Eva made the jam every season because the tree bore such a quantity of the purple-red fruit. She tried to think what to say to shield Johnathan.

'Louise . . .' Eva said again, imploring her to tell Mrs Burton.

'If you know anything, Louise, please tell me,' Julia said; 'it's not that I want to get the boy who split his lip punished— it's just that I've got to understand what's going on. You were at our place last week, Lou—you saw Bruce's black eye. He says that was from a fall—but his father didn't believe him then—and now, after last night, is certain it wasn't a fall. His father is very angry with him and feels there is more to this than we can see. We've gone along with Bruce—trying to do what we think is best for him, without forcing our way too hard. Perhaps that's been the trouble—we've handled him too gently.' Regret for something that could not be undone was in her voice.

'Dan's always said that he had to obey *his* father . . . willy-nilly. He says everyone needs discipline. Life will teach you, if no one else does, he says. I think—Dan thinks—we've been wrong, Eva.'

Louise was suddenly sorry for Julia Burton—for the mistakes people could make, without knowing, by just being misguided. How did you guard against being misguided?

'Eva, *you* know what I mean,' Julia turned to her cleaning lady; 'you know what I'm feeling.'

Julia, of course, was referring to Eva as a mother but how could Eva know a mother's feelings, or a daughter's for that

83

matter, when she was not a mother, thought Louise, with sudden anger.

'This is a crisis, Eva . . . I know. Dan's been very tolerant up to date. But now I'm afraid of what is going to happen. He's got it into his head that Bruce is in some kind of gang. Louise . . . you can see why I have to know.'

In some kind of gang. How deep was the hurt to a woman like Julia to have to say this of her son? Louise knew a brief moment of wonder as to whether Julia would have made that admission to anyone else in this town—to the doctor's wife, to the minister's wife, to the wives of any of the present-day holders of the big pastoral names. Or could she say such things in this cottage, because here there was no social level; where she could expect, maybe, there would be understanding? Yet Louise had to admit to herself that Julia was eschewing humbug and being straightforward.

'I don't know what it's all about,' Louise said, starting to eat the toast without even noticing the mulberry jam; 'I can't help you.'

She sat on the kitchen stool, close to the stove and was glad to be able to give her attention to her toast. She was remembering last week, and Bruce taking a kick at Johnathan. But she couldn't tell that to Bruce's mother. She felt only contempt for Bruce but although she resented the red dress and the two summer dresses and had once said 'Pigs to her!' she admired Julia Burton and, as Sheila's mother, liked her very much. She was grateful to her for having shown her some of the finer points of living, for having enabled her to see how wide a canvas life could fill. But she couldn't involve Johnathan.

'Tell me this . . .' said Julia, 'what girl was he with?'

'Diane . . . Diane Stone.'

'I know her,' sighed Julia; 'a tall, fair girl. Her parents have a good farm, out a bit, lots of money; she wears expensive clothes.'

'Yes . . . that's her.' And Louise had to hold back a smile at the memory of Mrs Pinkerton's 40-inch-bust cardigan.

'He has expensive tastes,' said Julia of her son, and began to drink the fresh cup of tea that Eva had made and, wordlessly, pushed towards her. This was the gesture of one mother to

84

another. On Monday when Eva was polishing the kitchen floor of the bank, she would tell Julia of Louise's threat to leave her and go to the city. She had refrained all the week from telling her, in case it should spark off some reference to the red dress. But now with Julia coming to the cottage with her worries, she could not hold back on her own troubles. They might both find a solution; though she would omit the part played by the red dress.

Mrs Burton drank her tea slowly. She had left Bruce back in bed again after the early morning visit to the doctor to get his lip stitched, and she wasn't eager to hurry back to Dan who was so unusually explosive.

From where she sat she could see the thickness of the stone walls of the original two rooms of the cottage, and through the open door of Louise's bedroom the cedar chest on the end wall; in the other direction she could see the living-room fireplace and the iron fender and set of fire-irons, a hundred years old perhaps, that stood on the hearth.

'You've not heard any more about the painting, I suppose, Eva?' she said.

'No. Senior-Constable Hennessy went all over this house looking for fingerprints. Nice man. He had a cup of tea with me. But he didn't find a thing. Only mine and Louise's prints on everything.'

'It's a shame. It may have been valuable, Eva. There's been a Chinese man—from Canton or Hong Kong or somewhere—in the bank a few times this week.'

'Oh-h . . .' Eva was interested, and glad to have the conversation switched from Bruce and Johnathan. If Louise wasn't going to come out openly with what she knew, then it was best to let the matter drop out of sight.

'He saw the description of the painting in the newspaper—and told Dan it could be worth something.'

Louise began somewhat noisily to clear the dirty dishes from the table and to carry them to the stretch of bench on the left-hand side of the sink. It seemed that one boulder after another was determined to drop on her head this morning. First Johnathan and now the painting.

'What is the Chinese man here for?' asked Eva.

'His grandfather was a digger—one of the lucky ones. The family started up a business of some kind in Hong Kong, and his grandson—an old man himself now—carries it on. He told Dan he often visits Australia on business and this time decided to make a trip to the goldfields—a sentimental journey, it seems.'

'I'd like to talk to him,' said Eva, 'I could tell him a lot about the painting.'

If Julia hadn't been there, Louise would have asked her aunt if she would tell about great-grandfather William peeking in at dead Chan Ah-Foo, huddled up in his bunk with his opium pipe beside him, quite dead; and removing the painting for safety. To all appearances of course, great-grandfather had now been proved right, the painting had been valuable enough to warrant safe keeping.

'I don't know whether he's still in the town,' said Julia. 'Dan will know—and where he's staying. I'll ask Dan. And now I'd better go.'

Though worried and miserable over her son, Julia was a fine-looking woman as she stood up. Her well-cut slacks and jacket suited her slimness and her pale skin was slightly pink from worry or the heat of the fire stove. She was a beautiful woman, Louise thought, and was suddenly sorry that she wasn't able to feel gratitude for the red dress. She didn't think now that Julia had given her the dress for any other reason than to be a help. At the same time, it meant that she placed Louise in the same category as Eva.

Julia walked though the living-room and Eva opened the front door for her. It was not often that a good car, shining clean, stood outside the cottage. The O'Gradys, who lived in the third of the three cottages, owned an old round-backed Vanguard but it was too old to bother to clean. Even Louise followed to savour the closeness of the car. Everyone had cars these days. Most families had two. But Eva would never have one and she, Louise, would not have one until she had earned enough to pay for it herself. She often dreamed of sitting behind a wheel, and the trees flying past.

They walked down the path singly and suddenly Johnathan appeared from the other side of the car. He had a self-conscious grin as he said; 'I had to look at it—latest model, isn't it? A beaut!'

Louise saw at once that he had her cardigan over his arm, and that his left eye was ringed with yellow-blue skin, as Bruce's had been last week.

'The kids are on their way,' he told Louise; 'I left a few minutes ahead of them . . . to go to the hall and get your cardigan.'

Eva said primly, and with astonishing command of the situation. 'This is Mrs Burton, Johnathan—Bruce's mother.'

Johnathan was certainly surprised to meet Bruce's mother, but he spoke very politely and without embarrassment when he said, 'How do you do, Mrs Burton.'

'Johnathan . . .? Are you Johnathan Baird?' said Julia.

CHAPTER ELEVEN

Louise never quite remembered how that situation was overcome. But it may have been because Andrew, Michael and Beth arrived at that very moment. They came noisily. Andrew had been pretending he was an aeroplane ever since leaving home because a jet had gone over just as they left the Corner Store, and so he immediately became its pilot and zoomed and streaked all the way to the cottage. He worried Beth as he was carrying the bag of ferreting nets, including a miner's pick, and Johnathan would be annoyed if the nets became unrolled and tangled. Beth carried the lunch and Michael the ferret box. Michael knew she detested the smell that came out of the box and stayed close to her, hoping in this way to exhort a sandwich before it was time. But she stood firm.

Beth was only a year older but she could cope, most times, with her brothers. As long as they didn't get a wattle switch and attack the calves of her legs. Her calves were of a tender variety—much more so, she knew, than anyone else's for she had experimented on girls at school. She hated wattle switches or even flicks with the tea-towel. Most of the time she tried not to let her brothers know how it hurt, aware that they would torment her all the more. There were wattles along the way this morning but fortunately planes and something to eat crowded out more sadistic thoughts.

They turned the corner of the cottage fence and whooped down on the car, and began savouring it with dirty fingers, even though Mrs Burton was there.

Louise said sharply, 'Don't muddy it up—it's clean.'

'Wheels aren't,' said Andrew; 'why didn't she clean the wheels, too?'

'They've just come up this muddy track,' said Louise.

'She shouldn't have driven through the puddles,' said Michael, 'if she wants to keep it clean.'

'Lay off!' said Johnathan as Michael ran his hand across the smooth velvety paintwork of the bonnet.

'Better'n our ute,' said Andrew.

'I'll go now,' Julia said to Eva. Julia had been staring at Johnathan's yellow eye, at the screwed-up cardigan he carried over his arm as though he wanted to disguise it, at Louise's red face. 'I must get back and see that Bruce stays in bed. We'll have a talk later.'

She got into her shining car, her lips angry, and not smiling at Louise as she nodded goodbye. She had to reverse on to the road because the builders of the cottage had not left a wide enough space between the cottage and the edge of the pad that fell away into the knobs and bumps of Ginger Gully. Johnathan's brothers and sister were a worry to her as they ran about the car, laughing when the wheels didn't grip in the yellow clay puddles and shouting their own advice to her.

'I'm ready to go,' Louise told Johnathan quickly, 'except for some lunch.'

'We've got enough to eat,' said Johnathan, aware that Eva was looking blackly at him. He believed it was his yellow eye and knew he looked like the devil, and so was eager to get away from her.

'Louise . . .' began her aunt.

'We're going now,' said Louise, 'I'll make my bed when I come back.'

She knew that it was only the presence of the younger children that stopped Eva from ordering her to stay home. Eva wouldn't run the risk of a confrontation on the clay track, in front of the miner's cottage, and with Mrs O'Grady out now at her front gate, also interested in the unusual activity. Mrs O'Grady called out to Eva. 'Mrs Burton, eh? She doesn't often come this way.'

'No,' said Eva, and lied; 'she wants me to start early on Monday.'

'So that's what she was after. Nice car she drives.'

And Mrs O'Grady went back into her cottage to stoke the stove. This morning she wanted to make some scones. Her daughter and her family were coming in for tea. So she didn't ask any more questions of Eva.

Eva stood looking after the young ones as they headed out over the pitted gully, running and hopping across the rough terrain, sure as rock wallabies. She was very angry with Louise. The girl had deliberately refrained from telling her employer what had happened at the dance. Now Mrs Burton would think that she, Eva, had held back, for she would surely expect Louise to have told her aunt about a fight. Fights were still news. Eva remembered a fight of many years ago . . . when two boys had fought over Rosemary. Supposing Johnathan and Bruce had fought over Louise! She trembled. And then tried to think what young people did in their boy-girl affairs these days. They were so different. This was another reason why she must keep Lou with her. Look after her. But she was very angry with Louise and watched the young ones out of sight—noting that they never once looked back. There was only one thing for her to do now; she must go and apologise to Mrs Burton, and talk the matter over with her as far as they both knew the facts.

She would make the beds and do the dishes—which were Louise's jobs on Saturday mornings while she cleaned the house—and then go.

She went into Louise's room first and as it was the day for changing the sheets pulled the quilt and blankets off the bed. That was when she saw Rosemary's suitcase, just under the edge of the bed. Rosemary had used the suitcase on her few trips to the city before she was married and as a rule it was stored out in the shed, wrapped in a piece of canvas.

Eva dragged it out, wondering, and when she opened it and saw Louise's clothes, neatly folded and stacked, she sat on the edge of the bed and cried.

'We'll head for the Ovens again,' Johnathan said, as they went their way through the scarred gully. Before the gold-rush a gentle creek had sung through here, and the roots of messmate had reinforced the banks where platypus had burrowed. But when man took over the burrowing, the stream had had to find some other way to the river, for the tossing and lumping of the earth left it without a course. Its way was devious now. It didn't sing through the gully any more.

'Aw-w . . . why the Ovens again!' snorted Michael. 'Didn't get one rabbit there last week. Let's go down to the river. We could give the ferrets a swim. I like to see 'em swim.'

'Then you'd be carrying them cooped up in their box with wet fur,' said Johnathan. 'It's bad for them to be cooped up wet, you know well enough.'

'They'll rub themselves dry on the grass,' protested Michael, 'and I could finish 'em off with my hanky.'

'And smell like dead meat for ever after,' said Beth.

'What's that got to do with you?' came in Andrew. 'They're our ferrets and if we want to smell like blowed meat . . .'

Beth wrinkled her nose. 'Gee . . . you're crude. I didn't say that.'

'You did—you know you did! cackled Michael.

'Yeah . . . crawling . . .' said Andrew.

'You're mad,' said Beth.

'Anyway, I want to give our two jacks a swim—let's go to the river.'

They both turned quickly to head to the right.

'Come back!' ordered Johnathan. 'We're going to the Ovens. And I'll stay with you long enough today to see that you get your nets set right—no stones or sticks to snag the thing when it rolls up.'

'We had 'em right last week.'

'The bunny got away,' Beth reminded them.

'Aw-w—you always side with him. *You two!*' Michael was disgusted. 'If he told you to unscrew your head you'd do it.'

'Gee! she'd look beaut!' screamed Andrew; 'just legs an' arms an' a middle—walking around . . . wouldn't be able to be always telling a bloke what to do.'

'Have to put a cork on the top,' frowned Andrew, 'how else would everything keep in?'

And while the two boys discussed this point, Louise took the opportunity to say to Johnathan, 'Aren't you going to stay with us *all* day?'

'No—have to go to Quin's again.'

'Do you have to go every week-end?'

'Well—lately, I have.'

'Does your mother have a message for the old bloke every week-end?'

'Well-l . . . let's just say . . . I have had to go there every week-end lately.'

They walked on. He should tell her, she thought fiercely. It was up to him to tell her what was going on now. He must have noted the angry way Julia Burton looked at him, and her aunt's dark look. So she said.

'Mrs Burton knows it was you who split Bruce's lip—he told her. She knew I was going to the dance and came to our place this morning to find out if I knew anything of what had happened.'

'So that explains why she couldn't take her eyes off *my* eye. I thought she was admiring the colour.'

'He told her you sprang at him out of the dark—that the attack was unprovoked.'

'Sounds like Bruce.'

'Johnathan—what is it? What is going on between you and that gang?'

She was sorry at once. She hadn't meant to ask straight out like that. Johnathan wasn't the kind of boy to be pressured. It was the impulsive streak in her—just as she had told Eva, on impulse, that she was leaving her.

'Going on? What d'ye mean?' Then he grinned. 'Maybe Bruce was right in what he told his mother. I did spring out at him from the dark. Did a real good Rugby tackle from the rear—only he knew I was coming. And he did have Dad's coat. Anyway, what else did she say?'

Louise told him. Not very willingly, but because she was relying on him for her fare to the city.

'So he needed a stitch in his lip, eh?—and she was going home to make sure he was staying in bed, not going specking or panning with the boys.' He seemed to be considering this situation.

'That's what she said.'

'Will he do as he's told?'

'He doesn't as a rule. But Mrs Burton says his old man is really mad with him. If the Tech finds he's in trouble again he might get expelled—so maybe he'll play it soft today.'

They walked on.

'I got Dad's coat brushed clean all right,' Johnathan said presently. 'But Mum asked a lot of silly questions about this eye. I don't think she believed a word I told her—how I fell off a chair and the leg came up and poked me in the eye. So . . . to square her . . . I said, if she wanted me to, I'd take another message to Quin.'

'And she did?'

'Yes. He's some sort of distant cousin. That's why she worries about him—feels that someone ought to go every week-end and make sure the old bloke is still alive. Must be grim living alone when you get old. Thinking perhaps you'll die alone.'

Louise turned away from that thought. Eva said something of this sort occasionally—about being alone.

'Johnathan . . .' she was a bit diffident, but there were details that had to be settled. 'Johnathan—I've been thinking—I'll go next Friday morning. Eva has a very full day on Friday—works at Dr Henshaw's place all day. She leaves an hour before me in the morning and never gets home until after six o'clock at night. Friday is Mrs Henshaw's solo afternoon and I think Eva stops late to get their dinner going. This means I can be in the city by eleven o'clock—that'll give me plenty of time to find a job and a boarding-house in the day.'

'Look here . . .!' Johnathan stopped walking, 'this is not going to work, y'know. It won't take the police twenty-four hours to find you and bring you back.'

'They won't even have to look for me!' said Louise scornfully. 'As soon as I've got both job and boarding-house, I'll let Eva know where I am. That'll keep the police out of it. It'll be between just me and Eva. By then it might have got through to her how I feel about the red dress and the way she likes being a cleaner . . . and doesn't want anything different.'

'And after that?'

'I'll play it by ear. But do you think . . . having got to the city . . . that I'll ever want to come back? Or will come back?'

'No,' said Johnathan, and remembered how pretty she had looked at the dance last night, even in the purple light, and how quick she always was to stand up for the loser. It was strange and contradictory to him that she thought of her aunt in this harsh way. Because it seemed to Johnathan—who knew a lot about apple-trees but not much about women, young or old, or even his mother to whom it was always so easy to talk—that Eva was a loser. Suddenly he felt guilty that he was going to help this girl escape from her to the city. He knew he was doing it mainly because he had definite ideas about shaping his own life and felt he was indebted to her enough to help her do the same.

'And about the money, Johnathan . . .?'

'I'll have it for you on Thursday,' he said shortly. So shortly that she knew it wasn't any use talking of her plans any more; that Johnathan didn't want to hear about her plans. Yet she badly wanted to talk of what she was going to do, how she was going to spend the money she earned, the life she was going to make for herself in the city. You needed to share what you did with someone. Otherwise it was only half living. But it was plain that Johnathan didn't want to hear.

As they had got away to such an early start, they took a longer route than last week, following for some distance the almost circular left curve of the old creek bed. The only water in the gully now was the rain-water trapped in those miner's holes shallow enough to have escaped bull-dozing when the deep ones had been made safe years ago, and from which frogs croaked as they passed. The ground was rough and red and bumpy but sprinkled, too, with the white crystals of shattered quartz.

The first diggers through here hadn't known much about quartz mining, even the quartz close to the surface, though they could see gold in the rock. But how to release it had been a technological difficulty which the early miners—shepherds, sailors, clerks, doctors, gentlemen, shop assistants—hadn't the time or the inclination to overcome. They sought the alluvial gold that weathering had already freed from the rock, the shining smooth golden pebbles and nuggets that could be washed and cradled from the earth. There was so much to be found in the alluvium that at first they had no need to bother about the quartz.

The Chinese fossickers, who could 'smell gold' and were indeed responsible for the discovery of the immensely rich *Canton* lode and the start of Ararat, had followed the European diggers along this creek and had taken the discarded rocky material and crushed it in their dolly-pots with a heavy hammer, earning riches for their employers back in Canton and sometimes for themselves, and leaving this dusting of white fragments like fat white sugar.

Louise dropped behind Johnathan. And now Chan Ah-Foo seemed to come close to her as she trod the ground where his countrymen had worked, back bent over cradle, washing, washing, washing, eye noting nothing but the gold caught in the hairy blanket or in the arms of the quicksilver; or hammering stolidly on the quartz stones in the dolly-pot. Never working with great haste, but working consistently. That was their secret . . . work, work, work . . . with time off perhaps for a pipe of opium; the opium that the European traders in the eighteenth century had introduced into China from India.

And back in Canton someone had received the gold.

But Chan Ah-Foo had stayed in *Hsin-chin-shan* too long—allowed himself to grow too old and to buy too many of the little brass boxes containing opium that could be purchased freely from the Chinese stores, so that he had neither the will nor the energy to return home to die. Now he was buried under the mess-mates.

Chan Ah-Foo may have worked on this very creek. Suddenly Louise was sure he had worked here—that he was in fact walking beside her. She could see him, in his pig-tail and coolie hat, and his smiling face.

95

They were a cheerful race, and the legend of their generosity had come down to her through Eva. But it must have been a monotonous lonely life with no wives or children. Some of them had lived here for thirty or forty years, with no kin—though they were a race whose social structure had been built on the family—and now there was little sign of them. Yet she felt Chan Ah-Foo at her side, jogging softly beside her in his embroidered wooden-soled slippers and white socks.

She began to feel very badly about the painting, almost as though Chan Ah-Foo's smile was an accusing smile. 'You broke it!—the story of the Seven Heavenly Sisters. And for what? To forsake your family duties?'

He asked the question so plainly that suddenly she had to get away from him and she ran to catch up with Johnathan. And to appease Chan Ah-Foo, she had to tell Johnathan about the picture. 'Great-grandfather William pinched it,' she said, out of breath, 'and I broke it.'

The story tumbled out of her so quickly, each word a bead of confession, that Johnathan just stood quietly on the very top of a red crag that looked like a termite castle but was simply the peculiar shape in which the last digger, perhaps a hundred years ago, had left his mullock heap.

'So the story in the paper wasn't true,' he said; 'the picture wasn't stolen . . . really.'

'The police had already been—the story had already gone to the paper—when I got home last Sunday,' Louise defended herself from those appraising eyes.

'I don't understand you, Louise,' Johnathan said. And meant exactly that. Because he didn't understand he offered no criticism, no censure, of what she had done, but he did say: 'Your aunt's going to be pretty upset when she hears about it.'

'She'll never hear about it . . . unless you tell her.'

'You know I'll never tell her,' he said quietly.

CHAPTER TWELVE

The young ones were far ahead now, running up and down the raggedy country, sometimes disappearing into the hollows of old mine workings, sometimes standing atop a pinnacle of red-brown gravel.

Although the tossed water-course wound an erratic way, each side was broken off sharply where the miners' picks had come to the end of the gold lead and ceased to tear down. From these edges, the country rolled away in paddocks of grass and trees; some of the gums were tall and spindly with several trunks stemming from the short-barrelled main trunk, like some hydra-headed aboreal freak, and others were rough-barked for ten feet and then emerged into smooth grey powerful trunks. Beneath all of them lay the brittle debris of leaves and spiky seed cups.

Some of the thick-trunked grey gums may have been standing when the first diggers came, not so tall then and with not as many gnarled knots to break the smoothness. But much of the growth would be of recent origin, for fire had ravaged this country at intervals—like the holocaust of 1851 when Victoria had burned almost from end to end—and even the fire of a year ago which had destroyed so much of the mining past.

While Louise and Johnathan were still far behind, Michael saw a rabbit disappear into a burrow beneath one of these trees close to the edge of the water-course. Here was a sure catch. No need to look for fresh scratchings or fresh droppings,

97

or a fox's scratch marks. And he dismissed from mind all the warnings that Johnathan had ever given him about putting ferrets into burrows that led under trees.

'The only time you put a ferret into that kind of burrow,' Johnathan had said, 'is when rabbits are as scarce as hens' teeth.'

But of course it was different when you actually saw a rabbit disappear into one of these holes, when you *knew* it was there, Michael reasoned; and Andrew, who was carrying the nets, and was right behind him, agreed entirely with his brother.

They were both a bit sensitive about not having made a catch last week, especially as Bluey Benn had caught a round dozen last Saturday; at forty cents a pair for good export grade carcasses that was $4.80. As Bluey had already repaid his father the cost of his ferrets his old man had let him keep the whole of the loot.

'We'll get this bloke in a tick . . . before Johnathan gets here,' Andrew said. 'He's too busy talking to that bird. Silly things—birds.'

He laid the canvas bag on the ground and pulled out the miner's pick, which was small enough to carry conveniently in the bag, and then the nets.

'We'll only need six—it's a small warren—only six holes,' said Michael.

His brother drew six nets from the bag, each neatly folded and tied up with its own drawstring. Johnathan always insisted that the nets be kept tidy and untangled, and had taken a great deal of trouble to explain to his young brothers just how to handle them.

Andrew quickly unrolled the first brown-coloured twine net—a brown net being considered better than a white one for catching a rabbit because the quarry couldn't distinguish so easily the danger across his hole. The boy stood on one leg as he thrust his other knee into the lower rounded edge as he had been taught to do, thereby giving that fold to the edge which first trapped the rabbit.

Five holes were covered and at the sixth, the one in which the rabbit had disappeared, Michael again opened the lid of the ferrets' box. He had already released one ferret into the first hole.

'Don't put both jacks in!' Beth warned quickly. 'Not under a tree—you might lose them both.'

But Michael had already grabbed the back of the neck of the second bundle of yellow-white fur. The little animal curled his body round almost in a half-circle and drew in his long claws. His pink damp nose quivered with excitement and tension, while his black eyes darted from side to side. His eyes were black because his parents had been of mixed colour, one black and one white, otherwise he would have had pink eyes as well as a pink nose.

Michael put him into the burrow and when the jack hesitated gave him a firm push. Then he arranged the net carefully over the hole, hanging it loosely from a point above, where the steel pin was driven into the ground. Both boys made sure that there were no sticks or stones to snag the net when the rabbit bolted into it.

'Should be quick,' Michael anticipated happily, and shouted an order to his sister. 'Get away from that hole, Beth—move up behind it.'

Beth didn't like ferrets or ferreting but she was quite familiar with the routine and had already moved out of sight-range of the burrows. She wasn't very interested in their catching a rabbit; she didn't eat rabbit, anyway.

'He'll bolt in a shake,' Michael said again, and stood expectant behind the main hole. The rabbit would not escape when the net tightened around him, but the boy had to be ready to catch the jack when he followed the rabbit out, though much more sedately.

They listened then to the underground rumbling that always followed the meeting of ferret and prey.

The ferrets were in, the nets were out, and the ferreters in position when Johnathan and Louise caught up.

Johnathan's anger burst like a bomb. 'Idiots! You've been told time and again! *Don't* put your ferrets into holes that go under a tree-trunk. If the trunk's a bit hollow more than likely the rabbit'll go up the trunk and the ferret after it. The rabbit can't get down—because the ferret's behind him—and the ferret won't come down because he's afraid of heights. He'll stay there until he dies.'

'Garn-n . . . they only go up sometimes,' said Michael, trying to pretend that he wasn't concerned that Johnathan had blown his top. 'They'll all be out in a minute.'

'I told them not to put both jacks in,' said Beth, primly.

'Now we sit and wait!' fumed Johnathan; 'and I wanted to get over to the Ovens by lunch-time, at least. We've already dawdled along the way.'

'Too right you have!' muttered Andrew, staring at Louise.

But Louise took no notice, her attention being on Johnathan who, she could see, had some particular reason for being irritated by this hold-up en route.

They sat around watching the burrows. There was no rumbling from underground now, all was extremely quiet.

'They've gone up all right!' said Jonathan at last, glumly eyeing the straight trunk of the grey gum. 'I can see a bit of a knot up about twelve feet—might be a hole there—maybe I could poke him down.'

'We haven't got a bunny yet,' protested Michael.

'You're not going to get one—that ferret's up the tree trunk, I bet. You won't see him again until I do something about it.'

Johnathan had to walk himself up the straight trunk of the grey gum, arms clasped around the trunk as he brought his knees up to his chin in a kind of caterpillar crawl. It was not an easy climb, but when he reached the black knot he was able to lever himself on to a nearby branch.

'Could be a hole here,' he called down, and that was when he pulled a red torch out of his jeans pocket and flashed it into the knot. 'No—not a real hole—just a bit of a cavity.'

He was disappointed and looked up for the next knot but it was many feet above him and even if there were a hole there, it would be impossible to poke a stick down far enough.

Preparing to descend, he thrust the torch towards the hip pocket of his jeans, and somehow the press-button caught on the taut edging of the pocket and whisked the flashlight out of his hand. It streaked red to the ground, striking a piece of quartz as it landed.

'Blast!' said Johnathan, and came down almost as quickly as his torch. He picked it up, to see that the globe was shattered. 'Blast!' he said again and was so angry that his face reddened from neck to forehead.

Whether it was to escape his brother's punishing hand or whether he felt he was doing something constructive, Michael at this moment lay down on the ground beside the burrow and pushed his arm in and upwards. He lay flat to give the utmost length to his skinny arm and screwed up his mouth and wrinkled his nose as he squiggled around to feel what might be in there.

When his fingers caught on fur he grunted satisfaction. 'Got it! Up on a kind of ledge!' And began to pull.

Then he gave a sudden yelp. 'Ow-w! Ouch-h!'

His body squirmed, his face whitened.

'It's got me! Something's got me! My arm . . . I can't get it out!'

Johnathan demanded. 'What's got you!'

'Something! It's got my arm . . . it's hanging on!'

Michael was biting his lip now and Johnathan began to beat the ground around the burrow with the pick handle, endeavouring to frighten what was in there.

Then suddenly the boy was free. He rolled away from the burrow, the right sleeve of his shirt and jumper ripped from elbow to wrist, and blood rapidly reddening the white shirt. Through the rent they could see the gashes of claw marks.

'Possum!' gasped Johnathan. 'There's a possum in there— one of the big grey bushies!'

Michael was staring at the blood. He had never seen so much of his own blood at one time before.

'Ow-w!' he said fascinated.

'Does it hurt?' said Andrew mesmerised.

'No,' said Michael, for the relief of the withdrawal of the claws had removed all sense of hurt.

Johnathan pushed back the two sleeves. 'Good long gashes,' he said, 'enough to make you bleed like a pig. But not really deep. You'll live, my boy.'

His own relief was in his light tone. He didn't particularly like the look of blood, either.

'We must tie it up,' said Louise, who had stood by saying

101

nothing, but was now suddenly practical. 'Anyone got a clean hanky?' Her own small handkerchief was clean but quite inadequate to cover such long scratches.

Between them they mustered enough linen to cover the scratches but the wound continued to bleed.

'You've got a lot of blood,' said Andrew admiringly.

'You'd better go home and get it tied up properly,' Johnathan was angry again. If the blooming kids would do as they were told this kind of thing wouldn't happen.

'Rotten old possum!' glared Michael.

'You can't blame the possum,' said Johnathan. 'The rabbit's dug under his tree—a nice dark hole right under the hollow middle of the trunk—and he's not against using a nice dry house. And you can't blame him for scratching back, either . . . if you pulled his tail.'

There were tufts of grey fur clinging to Michael's fingers. This was the result of a kind of escape mechanism a possum was able to use when a pursuing dog, for instance, managed to get close enough to take a snap at him. The fur came away easily into the dog's mouth, nearly choking him, and while he spluttered the possum whisked up his tree to safety.

Michael shook the fur away. 'What about my ferrets?'

'They must have the bunny lined up,' said Johnathan, 'and it must be one of the stubborn kind.'

But now there was a sudden flurry from the burrow from which Michael had just removed his arm, and out bolted an extremely frightened rabbit. He shot across Andrew's feet, past Beth and Louise and was lost immediately in the safety of the kangaroo grass beyond the warren.

Then came the two jacks, one behind the other, pattering out on their dainty feet, pink noses wrinkling after the smell of the rabbit.

Johnathan reached for the first one, the bigger of the two, and Andrew for the other, and they were quickly returned to their box. They immediately began to tumble and twist over each other in play, work forgotten.

'Thank goodness for that!' Johnathan said. 'Now you'd better get home Michael—you with him, Andrew.' He turned to Louise. 'Will you go with them, please—make sure they go home—and tell Mum what happened. I'll go on to Quin's and meet you at the Ovens in an hour or two. Will you do that, Louise? You and Beth.'

She knew that he was glad to be rid of his younger brothers and herself and Beth for an hour or two. She realised that he was using her in some way, for Michael's scratches weren't that bad, but she couldn't refuse. 'All right,' she said, 'see you at the Ovens later.'

Michael was still too interested in the red pattern on the rag to consider protest and, anyway, he was eager to get home to tell the story to Mum. He rather hoped that the shop would still be open—though it closed for lunch between twelve and two on Saturdays—so that he could tell some of the customers, as well.

Beth then gave Johnathan his share of the lunch, and four of them turned back, and one went forward.

As they turned round, Louise thought, 'Now, he'll have to tell me all about it.'

CHAPTER THIRTEEN

The two boys started to be a trouble as soon as they were out of sight of Johnathan. Although Michael kept admiring the bits of bandage with their splodges, he had already changed his mind about wanting to go home. And Andrew was complaining because he had to carry the net bag on his back and the ferret box in his hand. Not that the net bag was as heavy for Johnathan had kept the miner's pick.

'I shouldn't have to carry both,' he grumbled; 'Beth should carry the ferrets or the bag—one of 'em—and anyway Michael's left arm is all right.'

'Louise could carry the ferrets,' said Michael wickedly.

But Louise had no intention of carrying either ferrets or bag, both of which smelled. Nor would Beth. Ferrets, or ferreting, were not her delight, either.

All the way home the boys grumbled and loitered and threatened to take the ferrets to the river. Louise felt very old and churlish and hated them both especially as she had to bribe them with more than their fair share of the lunch to keep them on the track.

'The sooner we get home the sooner your mother can wash your arm,' she told Michael.

Which was the wrong thing to say for Michael wasn't looking forward to having his arm washed. It was comfortable now and he was beginning to think that he and Andrew had been a bit easy to agree to go home.

However, they did reach the Corner Store eventually and

went round the back because trading had ceased for Saturday lunch-time; being a Corner Store it would open again in the afternoon.

There was a fenced paddock stretching away behind the store, and Louise could see the sleek jersey cow that Johnathan had rescued, as a near-dead calf, from the railway-truck, and the half-dozen recently shorn sheep he had bought cheaply. Near to hand in the backyard were wooden fruit-cases, weathered to grey, and cardboard containers piled high, with the old grey ute standing in the middle. The present weather-board building, which was nearly a century old, had been built on the site of the original store of bark and saplings, and the back door opened directly from the kitchen into the yard.

Mrs Baird had heard them coming and was standing just inside the fly-wire door waiting for them. She was a plump comfortable-looking woman, but her hair was already grey and she was wrapped, like a sausage, in the blue overall she always wore in the shop. She opened the door and they filed through. The kitchen was very warm with a smell of soup from the big pot on the bricks at the side of the wood-fire stove. It was a room of things belonging to different people; a pipe, red knitting on the mantleshelf, bits of rope that boys use just inside the door, clothes airing on the clothes-horse pushed into the far corner, a brown earthenware bread crock, a dresser with crockery in assorted colours and patterns that a family is left with after years of breakages.

Beth told the tale with truth and no bias while Mrs Baird inspected Michael's arm. 'It's all right,' she said and poured some water from the steaming kettle into a basin, and got some clean rag.

'Hurry, mum,' said Michael, eyeing the basin.

'You're not going back,' said Mrs Baird; 'you know the rules about ferreting. You disobeyed. So you stay at home—both of you boys.'

Their bottom lips dropped in unison, their protests were noisy and, in the case of Andrew, expressed in an arm swung at Beth, taking care however not to make contact. 'Aw-w . . . her!' he blamed.

But Mrs Baird continued to wash the arm and Louise could see plainly that Johnathan's mother was a firm practical woman and that the two boys would spend the rest of the day at home. Because she could see that Mrs Baird was practical Louise felt concern for Johnathan and his future. Mrs Baird would surely find it hard to see a successful career for her eldest son in the depressed economic state of the orchard country. How would he overcome such firmness and practicality? Or would he?

But she was surprised when Beth came to her side and said, 'I'm not going back to the Ovens, either. Dora said she would come over to play if I were home this afternoon—only I didn't expect to be home—now I am. You can go back to Johnathan.'

Louise stared momentarily at the girl. She didn't know how but she saw that in some way she had qualified with Beth; qualified to keep her brother company. And she realised then that having all brothers and no sisters could deny a girl close contact with her own sex. Living only with brothers would be somewhat like living isolated as she, herself, did. Beth evidently felt some reaching out to her own kind, to this Dora, but had been ready to forego this satisfaction if her brother needed her. Now having seen that he had some contact with Louise, she was prepared to waive her right. Louise was surprised, because she had felt Beth's jealousy that first day.

As Louise crossed the back yard, Beth went with her, and when they were out of hearing from the kitchen, she said, 'If you can't find him, look out along White's Gully—the Brick Chimney end—that's where he'll be.'

'What doing?'

'I wouldn't know,' said Beth, flaring for a moment. Then she said, lip jutting a bit like Andrew's did sometimes, 'I wouldn't have told you—only I'd have got that rock down on me if it hadn't been for you. And . . . Johnathan seems to think you're all right.'

'Thanks,' said Louise.

'But wait at the Ovens for quite a bit,' Beth warned; 'Only then—if he doesn't come after a long time—try the Gully.'

As Louise said goodbye Beth looked uncertain as to whether

she had done the right thing; whether her trust in this girl who was her brother's friend would be justified. Funny that the kid should be grateful about the rock, Louise thought—she hadn't said anything at the time. Well, she would never want to tread on her heels again.

CHAPTER FOURTEEN

Louise walked quickly after she left the Corner Store. It was a long way back to the Ovens even by the shortest route. Johnathan was going to Quin's first but he should surely arrive at the Ovens before her. If he wasn't there, she wouldn't wait long before going to look for him, even though Beth had cautioned her to be patient. Obviously, Beth thought that if he didn't return in reasonable time, it was a matter for investigation; the thing she would do if she herself were waiting for him.

It was a day of pleasant sunshine and no wind, but Louise was tired and hot by the time she reached the Ovens, having hurried all the way. By this time, too, she was cross with Johnathan for, on the way, she had suddenly remembered the bundle of clothes under her bed, packed into the fibre suitcase that had been her mother's. If Eva took it into her head to make the bed and found the suitcase, she would know at once that she was planning to leave her very soon. And she would stupidly see something symbolic in that she was using Rosemary's suitcase, the one that had carried Rosemary's clothes to the city those few times so many years ago. The suitcase was still not shabby for it hadn't been used since.

Louise wished now that she hadn't come out with Johnathan today—what with Michael being silly enough to get scratched by the possum, and this long walk back. No wonder Mrs Baird hadn't let the kids come; they'd have been unbearable by now. She was hungry, too, for that greedy Michael had eaten most of her share of the lunch as well as his own.

There was no sign of Johnathan around the quartz kilns. A screwed-up lunch-paper showed where they had eaten last week, and there was the boulder that had fallen, caught in the cupped hollow at the bottom. Its track down the hill where it had flattened gorse and wattle sapling was marked with the withered growth. But a push couldn't overbalance it now, only centuries or a convulsive earth movement would release it from where it lay caught.

Louise didn't wait at all to see if Johnathan were coming. She decided to set out at once for Quin's and then, if he were not there, on to White's Gully. Both places were in the same direction although White's Gully was remote from any used track, a rubble-humped wasteland that few frequented these days.

She walked with some excitement now for, whatever happened, she was going to find out what Johnathan was up to.

Quin's cottage was isolated. At one time there had been a few others round about—miners' cottages of local stone put together with *pise*. When the occupants died or moved out, the dwellings were left to look after themselves and began to fall down. The bushfire of last year had finished them off. Now there were just some broken walls and a chimney stack or two. Old Quin's house stood because he lived in it and had fought the fire; and stopped leaks in the roof, and added a bit of modern cement to the wall when it looked as though another stone was going to fall out.

He was a fossicker; one of the few who remained in the district. Just an old, old man—near ninety—who preferred to fossick rather than take the pension. A false pride, a do-gooder said, who wanted to move him into the town so that he could die in a clean bed with white sheets. But Quin said that fossicking kept him alive. If he didn't take the pension he had to fossick to live. It was the sort of incentive that an old bloke needed. Every man needed to work, and what better reason to work, even at ninety, than to get the wherewithal to live?

It wasn't that he wanted to go on living forever, he always added. He believed, himself, that adventure could lie beyond the grave. But if he had to stay here a bit longer, he might as well be doing something.

109

Quin's cottage was not falling down but no one could say that he kept it over clean. He had a few cats and Dawn, the three-legged dog, all of which shared his shelter, while his ferrets weren't too far from the back door. A much earlier owner had planted a garden around the two-roomed cottage and outlined the flower-beds in dry ginger-beer bottles— brown stone bottles with the bottoms upended. You could just glimpse them here and there between the overhang of garden, which was all in a tangle, like his wild hair after he woke from sleep.

There was a bit of a canopy over his front door which faced west, and a weathered cane chair stood on a raised platform that someone might once have called a porch. A rose vine with half-inch curved thorns and scarcely any leaves climbed up one post and on to the roof where it lay coiled in inch-thick tendrils, like some strange emaciated snake.

Old Quin was sitting on his chair in the sun and watched Louise walk towards him. The bit of fenced ground around his cottage was not large because it had been the early custom to put a fence quite close around a house.

While Louise knew the old man by sight, she thought it unlikely that he would know her. He lived too much by himself and kept away from the townspeople.

He watched her come, not getting up, and she wondered if he would be pleased or not to see her. He wouldn't have many visitors out here; in fact, from all she heard, Johnathan would be his most regular visitor.

But when she opened the wooden gate from which the paint had fallen off decades ago, he did start to get up out of his chair. But she could see that he was stiff, even for a fossicker, and had difficulty in moving.

'Don't get up,' she said quickly.

'Who are you?'

He didn't wear glasses and his eyes looked at her on a very straight beam. But you could see they were old eyes by the same blue mistiness about them that distant mountains have.

'I'm Louise,' she said. 'My grandfather was Ed Turnbull.' She knew it was no use saying her father's name. He had been

110

quite unknown in the town, but Quin may have known grand-father Ed.

'Ed Turnbull, eh?—so you're his granddaughter. And great-granddaughter of William?'

'Yes.'

'I used to hear stories of that William. He was a bloke who liked to test his gun every evening at sunset and gave up wearing a sleeping-cap with his nightshirt, because he reckoned it wasn't necessary to keep the head warm at night in Australia. I do believe he started the fashion on the goldfields of no sleeping-cap at night.'

Louise was surprised that a man even as old as Quin should have heard stories about great-grandfather William.

'An' I knew Ed—worked down in the old Quartz Hole, didn't he? Always an underground man—until the fracture smoke and the dust from that sledge-hammer on rock got him. Not for me. I carted for the Quartz for forty years . . . but I stayed on the top. In the clean air. That's why I'll live to be a hundred. . . . So Ed Turnbull was *your* grandfather?'

'Yes, Mr Quin.'

Old Quin nodded his head and went on. 'He wasn't a bad sort of bloke. A bit hot-tempered at times, but not a bad bloke. 'You're his granddaughter—are you hot-tempered?'

'I don't know,' said Louise.

'Most likely you are,' said the old fellow. 'He'd flame like a torch . . . that Ed. And snuff it out as quickly—but only if you proved him wrong. Gosh, he'd hang on, like a mongrel dog, if he reckoned he was right. Are you like that?'

But Louise was getting impatient. 'Have you seen Johnathan, Mr Quin?'

'So that's why you came. You're after Johnathan. Not to see me?'

'Johnathan told me he was coming here first,' Louise said; 'then he was to meet me at the Ovens, but he didn't turn up.' She didn't add that she had waited only a minute.

'You're sure you didn't come to see *me?*' said the old man and screwed up the faded blue behind the eyelids. 'I been in demand this day.'

111

'Not really,' said Louise. 'I am looking for Johnathan.'

'Never had such traffic past the place . . . and *in* the place . . . and *on* the place . . . in years,' said old Quin settling comfortably into his chair. 'The first bloke to call asked if I'd give him a drink of water. I've never refused a bloke a drink of water yet, but when I come out with it, he'd gone.'

'First bloke . . .?'

'Young fellow. A bit older than Johnathan, maybe. Came before Johnathan. When Johnathan arrived he had a look around and said the bloke'd gone off with another of my bottles.'

'Bottles? What would he want with bottles?'

'To sell, I'm told. One of those from the border around the garden. Only there ain't no garden, really, and I ain't seen 'em—the bottles that is—in years. Can't crawl in myself under that rose. But it's nice in summertime—smells good. I'm not going to dig it out. We've grown old together—me and that rose.'

'What did he look like—the first boy? asked Louise.

'Oh . . . comic—a bit of sticking plaster or the like on his top lip. Seemed surprised to see me sitting here on me porch— I generally get a lift into town with McHale over the ridge on a Saturday morning. But McHale wasn't going today. So I was sitting here. When he asked me for a drink of water, I went in to get it for him. He looked thirsty. . . . I don't reckon it matters about no bottles. Anyway, I'm no bottle-oh. Stone-ginger bottles at that. I like the *yellow* gold.'

The old man settled further in his cane chair, looking a powerful man when you saw only those shoulders, and eyed the girl quizzically. '*You* don't want a drink of water, eh? Cool as ice, it is—I bring it up from the underground well with me pump. And you could pinch a bottle, too—if you wanted it. I wouldn't look.'

The old man seemed to find great amusement in what he was saying and cackled behind a blotched hand.

'No—I'm only looking for Johnathan,' Louise said. 'How long after Br . . . after the other boy . . . did he get here?'

'Oh . . . soon after, I'd say. Didn't really notice.'

'And how long has Johnathan been gone?'

'Oh-h . . . I don't know. I've been sitting here awhile since he went.'

'Where did he go?'

The old man looked at her very straight.

'I don't know.'

'Well—which way?'

'I didn't watch him go,' old Quin said. 'He just went. Just went. That's all. Except . . .'

'Except what?'

'Well, that stinking, feverish, moth-eaten mongrel that someone called Dawn . . .'

'Your three-legged dog?'

'Yes—me three-legged dog—she took off after him. On her three legs. He wouldn't know she was with him until they was half-a-mile away. She likes that boy. Smooges up to him when he comes. Reckon she knows he's still young . . . like herself . . . and can do sort of exciting things for a dog. Even a three-legged one.'

'And she hasn't come back?'

'Not yet. But she will. At dark, maybe. Funny dog. I've never known her stay away from me at night. Sleeps on the end of me bed—and sometimes under the bedclothes if it's cold enough. Puts her legless rump down on the softest part of the mattress and snores worse'n me.'

He laughed again. 'I don't blame her going off for a walk with Johnathan. He likes her and she likes him. But she likes me best—always comes back to me. Sit down and I'll tell you about her.'

'No, I have to go,' said Louise; 'I've got to find Johnathan. Are you sure you don't know which way he went?'

'Maybe that way . . .' said the old man and he pointed to a hill behind which, some distance across country, lay the town. It was the opposite direction from White's Gully. So she wasn't going to get anything out of old Quin!

'Goodbye,' she said, shutting the gate carefully, 'I hope Dawn gets back all right tonight.'

Louise walked very quickly after she left old Quin. For his

benefit, she started off in the direction of the town but once out of his sight, she swung around a knoll and headed for White's Gully.

White's Gully was only a couple of knobby hills away from Quin's cottage. A hundred years ago these hills would have been forested with mess-mate and stringybark and sheoak, but the diggers had cut down the trees for wood for their fires, for sawn lengths for their rough shelters, and timbering for their shafts. These ridges and the gully itself were bald now except for some patchy growth that had appeared this spring.

Last summer this gully had been an inferno—a great river of flame. Trees had exploded like fire-crackers and 'spot' fires had hurled from knoll to knoll, landing in other gullies, miles away, to start fresh fires. When the last flame had guttered out there was little left in the gully except ash. But potash makes a rich pasture and where the diggers had not exposed the entrails of the earth, on which nothing grew, kangaroo grass was now knee-high and would soon turn yellow in summer heat.

The gully itself was like Ginger Gully. It twisted and turned with the lie of the land and the old creek bed. There was water, in fact, trickling through here, taking a very devious course, going underground at times, but always flowing—a shallow stream of cold, clear water.

There were the same hillocks and mounds and holes, the man-made pads where, during the heyday of mining, men with a sense of more dependable money-making, had banked and levelled the discarded mullock and erected a store or a sly-grog shop in the very midst of the diggings. Now a bit of iron, twisted grotesquely, on such a site was all that remained of store or grog-shop. In time, fires and weathering would eventually remove forever the last evidence that remained of the gold-diggers.

It was just as Louise was nearing one of these levelled platforms that she glimpsed a figure moving on the other side. She saw it was a boy and hurried, running lightly over the pebbled ground. She began to call 'Johnathan! Johnathan! Wait!'

There was no reply and she called again. Her voice was not built for volume and the high scratchy note embarrassed her. Why didn't he answer? He couldn't help but hear on such a still quiet day.

'Johnathan!'

But still no answer. She stopped running then, to silence the noise of disturbed pebble and stone, and went forward very quietly. If he wasn't going to answer her, and didn't want her to find him, she would try to stalk him. He was there all right. She had glimpsed him. Having changed her strategy, she made use now of all the high mounds, moving forward around the levelled ground as noiselessly as an Aboriginal stalking a kangaroo. But she felt ridiculous, and very angry.

Then she came upon her quarry, squatting behind a red hillock. There was a piece of sticking-plaster on his upper lip.

'Bruce!'

They confronted each other.

He stood up and she could see that he was still arrogant and insolent and assured, despite the cut lip.

'So you're looking for Johnathan,' he said, 'and all you find is me.'

'What are you doing here! You're supposed to be home in bed!'

'What! Keeping a cut lip warm!'

'Your mother . . .'

'Yes, I know she went to see your aunt, and asked a lot of questions. And I know that your answers didn't please her. It was because she wasn't pleased that I was able to get her to tell me where she'd been. She happened to tell me, too, that you and Johnathan were going on safari today—so here I am. I thought it would be interesting.'

'Where's the rest of them?'

'My mates?' he raised well-formed eyebrows. 'Oh . . . sometimes I operate alone—it's more profitable.'

She saw then that there were two stone ginger-beer bottles on the ground at his feet.

He followed her glance and said easily; 'Old Quin gave them to me. Worth a dollar or two each as antiques—depends

115

where you sell them. Handy for a bloke like me without any pocket money.'

Her eyes queried him. 'Yes. Didn't you know? The old man stopped my pocket money . . . end of last term. Not doing well enough to be worth pocket money, he said. They were both rather pleased though when I decided to go panning—they felt I was responding to their tactics. Even reckoned I was showing initiative.'

'They don't really know you, do they?' said Louise.

He laughed and went on. 'But panning's too back-breaking— too slow—for me. And I ask you, how is a bloke to get on with the birds if he hasn't got enough of the doings in his pocket? Besides, I'm all for getting what you can when you can— mightn't be around tomorrow. And you girls like money spent on you—so I was glad to meet up with old Quin.'

Anger burned Louise. All girls shouldn't be lumped together like this—taken for granted! She would be bitterly humiliated if a boy stole so that he could impress her.

'Quin *gave* them to you?'

'Of course. You don't think I'd steal them from an old bloke like Quin, do you? And me being Sheila's brother?'

If he hadn't added that last remark, she might have believed him.

'What have you done to Johnathan?' she demanded.

'Done to Johnathan? Not a thing. I haven't found him yet. When I heard you call—I thought I was in luck. Here's his girl-friend, I said to myself. She'll lead me to him—instead of which she found me. Anyway, where *is* Johnathan?'

'I don't know.'

'No, I suppose you don't. You wouldn't have been calling out to me—thinking I was him—if you'd known just where he is. But at least he's somewhere about. I'm sure of that now.'

'I'm going home,' said Louise. 'I've no idea where Johnathan is. When I glimpsed you—I just thought it might be him.'

She began to turn and then a dog barked. Not a wild, angry bark, or an excited bark, or a gay bark, but just a questing, questioning sort of bark. It was not very close, further up the gully, probably around a bend or two.

116

'A dog—maybe Johnathan's with him,' Bruce said.

'Johnathan hasn't got a dog.'

'He could have picked one up . . . along the track,' said Bruce, and turned quickly in the direction of the sound.

The dog barked again, a half-hearted bark as if he were disappointed about something, and Louise followed Bruce.

CHAPTER FIFTEEN

Louise followed Bruce across the lumpy and bumpy ground. She had to see what he saw.

And there was Dawn standing on her three legs and barking with her head lowered, her tail balancing her, so that she could look down on something below. She was standing on a raised but flat section of gravelly ground, like the platform they had just left, but the hole . . . or whatever it was . . . was on the far side from them. They couldn't see what she was barking at.

Bruce reached the spot first, and he was smiling by the time Louise caught up. They both looked down into what appeared to be a square underground bricked-in room whose roof had partly fallen in. The top rows of bricks of the four walls were plainly visible and the sheets of iron that had formed the roof or ceiling, probably over a framework of heavy wooden beams, were protruding through the thin layer of earth that had evidently been placed, for coolness, on top of the iron. At one corner, the iron had been levered aside, recently it appeared, allowing entry and light to whatever lay below.

'An old cellar!' cried Bruce, with great satisfaction. 'Burnt bricks, see! Burnt more than once, I'd say. Could have been a Chinese store and grog-shop on this spot. Last year's fire must have uncovered the old cellar.'

With Dawn performing on the bank, it was plain that Johnathan was below, that he had entered through the narrow opening. And Dawn hadn't been able to go down with him because a dog needed four legs for that kind of scrabbling. Now she was telling Johnathan that she was tired of being without him on the surface.

She noted the arrival of Louise and Bruce with a sideways look and a half-wag of the tail, but her concentration was for the boy she could not see. She wanted to go down there with him, or have him come up to her.

'Knew Johnathan was up to something—the way he's been nosing around!' Bruce exulted.

'And you nosing after him!'

'Of course!' And Bruce added enviously, 'It's handy for him having old Quin as a relative, with the old boy always fossicking about, turning over things. I've been visiting Quin myself whenever I could, hoping he'd let slip a word—but he's too fly—and keeping my eye on Johnathan.'

'Setting your mates to keep an eye on him, too,' said Louise angrily.

'Of course! I . . . we, that is . . . aimed to find whatever there was to find . . . first. No matter . . . this'll be a job for both me *and my mates*.'

Louise knew what he meant. They would use force to keep Johnathan away from his find.

'Should be some good stuff down there!' Bruce was very excited. 'Old bottles and jars—a hundred years or more old. Some of the Chinese ginger jars bring a good price and there should be all sorts of European bottles. Maybe a Munro's whisky or a blue castor-oil bottle—worth twelve dollars. I wouldn't give them house room myself, but they're good for cash all right. All these old bottles that the diggers chucked away—call 'em antiques now. My mother's made a study of this sort of thing—smart thing to do today. I've learned a lot from her—more than she thinks.'

Louise stared at him. Surely this greedy, grasping youth, with his cut lip, wasn't Julia's son, Sheila's brother?

'I'll go back to town now and collect my mates—we'll soon get what we want out of that hole. Or at least *they* can go down for me—not keen on dark holes myself. Never played in the mines even when I was a youngster—couldn't stand the idea

of the weight of the earth on top of me. Never make a miner . . .
me! But the boys'll go down.'

'It's Johnathan's find!'

'Only as long as he can keep it!' said Bruce. 'I got some
information out of old Quin—but not quite enough. Though
it brought me to where you found me. I'd have got on to it
this afternoon. Now I must get back—and get the boys. Better
tell Johnathan to be gone by the time we arrive.'

'It's Johnathan's!' cried Louise.

Bruce leered at her, looking anything but handsome with
that cut lip. 'Interested yourself, eh? Was he going to give you
some money to run away . . . to go to town?'

Louise stared at him.

'Just before I left this morning, I heard your aunt telling my
mother the whole sad, sad story . . . about how she'd found
your clothes packed. They were consoling each other. And were
so wrapped up in their children and their problems that this
child was able to slip out of the house without anyone noticing
him go. The whole thing worked out very well.'

He smiled comfortably.

'Sheila's got a rotten brother!' she cried.

'You're the only girl who doesn't like me,' said Bruce;
'most of them go for me in a big way. Why don't you get to
know me . . . eh? You'd find that I'm much more interesting
than that Johnathan, he hasn't grown-up yet. And I might
find you interesting, too. You've got more oomph than shows
up at first sight. What about it?'

It was then that some of the hot temper that had been her
grandfather's but which seldom ignited in her, flared like a
torch and forgetting that Bruce already had a cut lip, she took
a smack at his face. Not a gentle smack but a lunge and a
wallop with all the force of her strong right arm.

Bruce remembered his lip and stepped back smartly. He
didn't want any more stitches. But he still caught most of
the blow.

And he didn't know that here the brick retaining wall of
the cellar was only holding because of the formation of brick
upon brick; he didn't know that the *pise* binding the bricks

together had been reduced to dust by the last fire; or that the iron itself had been rendered paper thin by that same holocaust.

He somersaulted heavily backwards, falling straight through the iron with its light covering of gravel . . . and Louise fell after him.

The wall collapsed and tons of the bank with it. It fell on the remaining roof bearing it down in a kind of slow motion but with irresistible certainty. And because the wall forming the angle was no less weak and needed only a start—as Beth's boulder had needed only a start—it fell too, and dragged a good portion of the third wall with it.

Louise and Bruce would have been buried at once under many tons of debris if some of the blackened wooden timbers, which had been protected somewhat from the fire by the covering of iron and earth, had not fallen across at an angle and jabbed their ends into the earthen floor. A few sheets of the iron caught on the timber and held back the rubble.

When the rumbling ceased the two were lying flat . . . under the protective covering of the beam. But the darkness was blackness. And with all that jumble of gravel and stone and earth above them, they couldn't even hear the barking of the three-legged dog who, somehow, had propped backwards on her three legs and not followed them into the darkness.

Louise could not even make a cry. With the breath knocked out of her, with the feeling that the earth had opened and swallowed her, with the conviction that she had plunged from the warmth of daylight into her tomb, she lay there waiting for the darkness itself to do something, to finish her off.

Then she felt movement under her left leg and remembered Bruce.

There came a loud shuddering breath 'Louise . . . are you there, Louise?'

She couldn't answer, because she had no breath and no words.

'Louise! Louise-e! Are you dead?' There was the very fear of hell in the voice, the terrible burgeoning fear of one who fears the unknown.

'Louise-e!'

And still the girl could not answer.

121

The darkness was thick and the blanketing weight of earth that covered them was a blanket that smelled of the mysterious, frightening insides of that earth.

'Louise-e!' And now the voice was that of one who knows he is dead, yet is alive to know it.

Huskily she managed 'I'm here . . .'

But it was not the voice that was like the voice Bruce knew; it was the voice of his companion in death. It was very faint and far-away, even though it was close, and it was as frightening as the darkness. Because now, suddenly, it seemed to him that it would be better if she were dead than so injured that he would have to listen to her die all over again. Suddenly he wanted her to be dead for she would be too great a responsibility to him if she were still alive.

'I'm here . . .' she said again.

But he didn't reply because he was afraid of what she would say next.

'Are you hurt, Bruce?' The voice was stronger. 'Can you move?'

The question was like a directive and he tried each limb in turn, both arms, both legs, his head. He was surprised that he could move all of them, that nothing was broken, but he waited for her to ask again 'Can you move?'

'Yes.'

'Nothing . . . nothing pressing on you?'

'No.'

'Same with me.'

He heard movement then, of hands questing in the darkness. Once her hand touched his and it frightened him with its burning heat, so that he nearly yelped.

'Some of the beams have fallen on the angle . . . and some of the iron has held in places . . .' Louise's voice was steadier now. 'It's saved us.'

Bruce laughed wildly. 'From what!'

'But I don't know about Johnathan—perhaps he's at the other end—crushed.'

And she called softly, 'Johnathan . . . Johnathan . . .' as if she didn't want to wake him if he were dead. Better for him to stay dead, quietly, if it were so. Much better—kinder—to be dead than alive . . . buried alive. Someone would dig them out in the end, of course; but not in time . . . she didn't believe it could possibly be in time.

But just to be sure about Johnathan she called again 'Johnathan . . .'

And now from behind her head, somewhere in the darkness, there came a scratching sound, a slithering sound, and the staccato of small stones slipping as though pressured under impatient feet. Yet it seemed more like a four-footed animal than a two-footed Johnathan.

She called again 'Johnathan . . .'

He answered her, from somewhere behind them. 'I'm here! I'm coming!'

And she immediately accepted the fact that he was not dead, but buried alive with them. 'Bruce is here, too,' she said, 'but he's not hurt—he can move his arms and legs.'

Nobody asked of the others what they were doing in this hole. They only knew that the way out to the sunshine and the howling dog—whose howls they could not hear—was cut off.

'Where are you?' asked Louise.

'I'm in a bit of a tunnel—leads away and down from the cellar.'

'Johnathan . . .' Louise said his name thankfully, realising now that there was an opening not far behind her head, and this must be in the fourth wall of the cellar which was evidently stronger than the rest and had remained partially intact.

'I heard the crash—like an explosion,' said Johnathan, 'and crawled back. You're in an old mine-shaft—bricked up for a cellar. There are several tunnels off it—I was lucky to be in this one when the thing collapsed.'

'Then there's a way out!' Bruce's voice was suddenly alive.

'I don't know.'

'But . . . but . . . at least we can get into the tunnel . . . away from this stuff that's hanging over us?'

'Yes—I think so—if you're not pinned anywhere. But you'll have to move very carefully in case you shift whatever is holding it up and it all comes down. It'll crash quickly if that happens.'

Bruce groaned then, and Louise wished that she had died in the first fall of earth. It was much worse waiting for the thing to crash, and crush, out of the darkness. She said, 'Have you got a light, Johnathan?'

'Only matches. Lost my torch over that possum—d'ye remember, Louise? Fortunately, I could see well enough in the cellar while the hole in the roof was there.'

Now they heard his fingers fumbling around all the things in his pocket. Then the tiny flame burst. It lit the sagging, splintered beam, and the narrow space in which they lay, faces upward, and feet furthest from Johnathan. The earth had smelled close but before the match died, it showed how very close, how perilously close, it was to face and body.

'Hell . . .' said Bruce, and shut his eyes.

'Start to move . . . on your backs,' said Johnathan; 'very gently—this way—towards my voice. Don't turn your shoulders —you might catch a broken bit of wood. It won't take much to move the lot. . . . I'll pull you backwards by the shoulders. Louise first . . . she's nearest me.'

'Hurry . . .' Bruce said.

'I can only pull quietly—and be careful of the way you move your feet. Now, Louise . . . very gently . . . gently . . . don't wiggle your feet!'

His hands were firm on her shoulders as he pulled her back . . . back . . . back into the darkness of his tunnel. She was glad of the feel of his hands, aware of their warmth, of their gentle urging. If it hadn't been for the darkness, and the chance that the debris would fall further, she could have wished that the comfort of his hands would hold her forever.

'I heard a creak . . . hurry!' whispered Bruce. 'The wood's moving!—felt it against my leg. Hurry!'

If the earth fell now, it would not be slow but quick, crushing and smothering.

'Hurry . . .'

'Louise is out—in the tunnel. I think I can just reach you. Ease to your right . . . gently . . . so I can get a grip on you. Don't turn over . . . there isn't room!'

'But I heard it creak again! it's about to go!'

'I've got you! Don't turn over! Your shoulders will catch the beam. I've got you. Just press back . . . gently . . . gently . . .'

As Johnathan pulled the older boy backwards, there was the sound of their breathing in the tunnel—the sound of three people breathing—deep, hard, hurting breaths. And the sound, too, of creaking . . . creaking . . . creaking . . . and the noisy bang as stones fell.

But Bruce had been in the tunnel a full minute before the beam gave way, leaving no cunning space beneath it in which to preserve the life of a girl or a boy.

They leaned against each other in the darkness, each seeking comfort from knowing that he was not alone, that there was the warmth of flesh and blood near even if he couldn't see it.

'Strike another match, Johnathan,' said Louise, aware that a long shudder was passing through Bruce, pressed close to her. She remembered that he had said he couldn't bear to go down into dark holes.

The match flared, revealing that the mouth of the tunnel into which they had escaped from the mine-shaft was now sealed off with rubble. In the final collapse much rock and gravel had spilled into this narrow passage-way and was still rolling lazily. They had a glimpse of the crystal lines of calcite in narrow seams or faults, and slight trickles of water. They saw a small white frog with bulbous glazed eyes, and a pulse in its neck thumping.

'It's not high enough to stand up in!' cried Bruce.

'No—and it gets lower as it goes in.'

'Where does it lead?'

'It peters out a hundred yards further in.'

'A dead end?'

'Yes. But there are two other tunnels leading off it on the right. One very short . . . another dead end. I haven't been along the second.'

'Strike another match,' ordered Bruce.

'I can't keep on striking matches. I've only this one box, and that's not full.'

'We are in the middle of the earth,' said the voice of Louise, low and wondering. 'Walled up . . . with white frogs.'

125

'Don't say it!' Bruce was rough. I can feel it . . . squeezing me in. Heavy on top of me. If only I could stand up. I've *got* to stand up.'

He tried to stretch full height, which was taller than Johnathan, and his companions knew he quickly bumped his head when a small rock fell.

'White frogs . . .' said Louise, voice low still, 'and it's black in here.'

'That's why the frogs are white,' said Johnathan.

'We won't know when they're going to crawl over us . . .'

'What if they do!' snapped the boy. 'Frogs are all right.'

'Yes . . . of course . . . a frog's all right . . . Only I wish they weren't white.'

The boys knew what she meant . . . that they had left the world of the normal for what, to them, was the abnormal.

'Snap out of it!' said Johnathan. 'A frog's a frog no matter what its colour.'

They were all quiet, still, with only a rolling stone making noise. So still they might have been as intangible as the dark.

Then Louise spoke, her voice normal; 'Are we going to try to get out, or wait until they dig us out, Johnathan?' she asked, practical again, but only because she felt detached as though she were talking about three people who were trapped in a tunnel. Not about herself and Johnathan and Bruce.

'We don't know about the air . . . how long it will last. Maybe long enough to be rescued.'

'Feels as though it's getting stuffy already,' said Bruce, and they heard him sniff, testing the air.

'Perhaps the second tunnel will lead us out,' said Louise; 'lots of the old shafts had two entrances.'

'Yes,' Johnathan agreed, 'but this gully has been turned over so much, the first shafts and tunnels have broken and filled in.'

'Without light we won't know if there are any holes in the floor,' Bruce said; 'sometimes the diggers sank a new shaft in the floor of a tunnel.'

'We can crawl carefully,' said Louise; 'and I think we should start now. We won't be able to settle down to wait to be dug out until we know we can't get out any other way.'

126

'You're right. We won't be missed until we don't turn up for tea . . . and then the searchers will have to find us.'

'They'll know we're in White's Gully—Beth knows.'

'She doesn't know the exact spot. And this Gully has a lot of turnings and twists—goes for a long way.'

'There's the dog on top,' said Bruce gladly.

'She will go home to old Quin at dusk,' said Louise.

'Yes—she always does,' agreed Johnathan. 'She likes to be with me—but she knows her real duty is to the old man.'

'Then we have a long time to wait to be dug out,' said the girl; 'so we had better try every way to get out ourselves. Don't you think that's wise, Bruce?'

She appealed to him because she knew, instinctively, that she had to bolster Bruce or he would crack long before they were rescued. And if one cracked, it would be so easy for the others to follow.

'Yes . . . yes . . . you're right.'

'I'll go ahead,' said Johnathan; 'I've got some idea where the bad patches are. You two keep close to the sides of the tunnel.'

There was the sound of movement now as Johnathan crawled forward into an almost touchable darkness, and Louise and Bruce kept close to either wall. Floor and wall were wet and cold. Now and again a leg or an arm made contact, for the tunnel was narrow, and Louise felt the vibration of tension in Bruce.

They passed the first blind lead-off, they negotiated the holes in the floor of the tunnel they were in and they came, at last, to the second turn-off.

Right from the start this tunnel was very much narrower and lower, so that they could proceed only in single file; nor was it a straight drive but twisted in several different directions.

'Reckon this has been an exploratory tunnel,' said Johnathan.

It was so low that men surely had worked in here on their knees. But at least these men had had candles set in a twist of wire—their 'spiders'. Light would have made all the difference. There was no living without light . . . except for the frog that could be carried as spawn into a cavity in the rock by water

127

seeping through and draw substance from the same source. Louise could hardly believe that she was alive in this darkness. There was nothing . . . nothing to see . . . not even her hand— only a darkness as thick as a woven black blanket.

They turned another of the corners and there ahead was a tiny slit of light, like an almond-shaped eye.

'An opening!' cried Louise. 'We can get out!'

'Yes—an opening,' Johnathan said, but flatly. 'A very small opening—which no doubt we could enlarge—if we can reach it.'

'What do you mean!'

'I've a feeling that the rest of this passage . . . leading to that opening . . . is not any sort of a miner's tunnel. I think it's a freak cavity brought about by all the movement that's gone on here.'

'But that doesn't matter, Johnathan! It doesn't matter what kind of tunnel it is—so long as we can get out!'

'I'll try it first,' Johnathan said; 'wait here. Don't follow . . . yet.'

They heard him move forward again in the darkness, saw his body blot out the eye of light ahead. They crouched so still themselves that they heard every movement that Johnathan made, even after he'd gone some distance ahead. They heard his breathing, the scraping of his shoes on the floor of the tunnel, the dislodgment of loose stones. They listened to these noises for a long time, it seemed, then Johnathan's voice floated back to them from a long way off.

'I'm coming back . . . and I'll have to come backwards—I can't turn round.'

Neither spoke, their disappointment was too great. They knew that Johnathan thought that the risk of getting through to that eye of light was greater than the risk of waiting at the tunnel-opening for rescue. He was breathing very hard when he joined them.

'I got to the stage where there was only room for my body . . . wriggling flat,' he said; 'and getting narrower. But the worst part is—it's not solid. I heard it talk.'

'What do you mean . . . "talk"?'

'The rock creaked—there are cracks in it—our own movements could bring the top in on us.'

128

They stayed very still . . . the three of them; and round about the unseen walls listened . . . the blanket woven of blackness listened . . . pebbles in the tunnel stayed still to listen . . . white frogs listened . . . all wondering what the three would do.

Louise wanted to stretch her shoulders wide . . . to stretch her arms as far as they would reach . . . to stretch her legs . . . even to stretch her throat in a scream. But she stayed still; and was thankful that the others stayed still . . . for there was no room in which to stretch or scream.

She said; 'Then we must go back to the mouth of the tunnel, and wait. They'll dig us out . . . in the end.'

CHAPTER SIXTEEN

It seemed to take a long time to get back to the blocked entrance of the tunnel. Louise hated turning her back on that slit of light, almond-shaped like a Chinese eye, but she knew that Johnathan's judgment was sound and he would not make such a decision unless he felt it was the right one.

Arms and legs were grazed in this journey through blackness, because even slow and cautious movement could not miss all the sharp projections or prevent some falling into holes, and Louise prayed that a hand or a foot wouldn't crush the bulbous glazed eyes of a frog. She was aware now of other cuts and bruises—sustained in the first fall—as well as being wet, cold and hungry.

The day had been so warm on the surface that she hadn't worn a cardigan over her cotton jeans and jumper, and she was hungry because Michael had eaten most of her lunch. It was Michael's fault, too, that the torch was broken and they had to rely on matches. Johnathan's brothers were awful kids.

At first the three had very little to say to each other. Now that they knew they had to wait, it seemed that time interminable stretched ahead. Each tried to make himself comfortable in his own separate way; legs stretched out, or curled up, backs against the rock wall. They sat apart at first but the boys were lightly clad, too, and the cold and wetness around them soon drew them to sit close together.

'Do you think we'll hear when they start to dig?' Louise said at last.

'I don't know,' said Johnathan; 'we're at least ten or twelve feet down.'

'I wonder will they start soon?'

'Not until well after dark—I'm sure of that.'

This sounded such a long way off, such a lot of time to be lived that Louise's whole body suddenly clamoured for action . . . action to fill in the time, to distract the thought. But the only action they could have was talk.

'Johnathan—what was in the cellar?'

'A lot of broken bottles.'

'Broken . . .?'

'Yes. I'd reckon that the bushfire that burned down the pub in the first place—in the digging days—broke a lot of them. The full ones that survived would have been retrieved then, but I'd hoped there would be a lot of empties left.'

'Like a Jamaica rum, 1860,' murmured Bruce.

'And there probably were until last year's burn—judging by the amount of broken glass.'

'Glass?' queried Louise. 'We didn't fall on any.'

'That was because I'd already swept it up into the far corner—beyond those fallen beams. I expected to be in and out of the cellar—I was going to dig over the floor for anything that might have become embedded—and wasn't very keen on working in a sea of broken glass. The only things left intact were a couple of heavy Chinese she-yah jars, a few stone-ginger bottles, and . . .'

'They're worth money,' Bruce interrupted.

'You ought to know,' Johnathan agreed drily. 'You've pinched a few here and there—mostly from old people like Quin who don't know they're worth a dollar or two. That old man could go out into his garden when he's too gouty to scrounge in the creek, and pull up enough stone-ginger bottles to keep him in tucker for weeks. And you have to pinch them!'

Johnathan sounded as though he was about to jump up and take a punch at Bruce, which brought Louise in.

'Quin said he wasn't a bottle-oh!' Then she changed the subject swiftly. 'You started to say there was something else in the cellar?'

131

'Yes. These two bullet bottles.'

There was the clink of glass on glass as Johnathan touched the bottles, resting in a niche in the wall behind him. 'Found them today—put them in this hole for safety. Just as well I did. Anything left in the cellar is flattened now.'

Louise and Bruce knew what a 'bullet' bottle was. It was a lemonade bottle of a century ago, with a bullet-nosed bottom instead of a round flat bottom. These particular lemonade bottles were made that way so that they would always have to lie on their sides, thereby keeping the cork wet and tight. As they were useless to stand on a shelf and become the receptacle for some other commodity, few had been preserved. They were sought by antique dealers or curiousity shops.

Louise steered the conversation again. 'Johnathan—how did you know the cellar was here?'

'Well, everybody knows and the old records show that where-ever there was a big rush, with thousands of men, there was a mushroom growth of stores. Old Quin has always kept his eyes open. He found the cellar a few weeks ago. Last summer's fire uncovered traces of it—burned off the gorse and peppercorns that had been hiding it. It was just lucky that no one discovered it before he did. Then he told me. But only after I'd promised to be careful the way I handled the timbering and iron. He reckoned it'd be rotten after a hundred years or so.'

'He shouldn't have told you—knowing the risk!' said Louise fiercely.

'He knows I want to make money. He thought I might find something interesting . . . valuable . . . in here. No good to him, of course. He can still puddle with a dish in a creek bed, but he can't climb in and out of shafts or deep holes. And he reckoned I had enough sense to take precautions. Only I was in a bit of a hurry.'

'You wanted to find something quickly . . . for money . . . like Bruce?' Louise said, her voice low even in the darkness.

'Yes,' said Johnathan drily, 'I wanted to find something quickly for money but not like Bruce.'

'For me?'

Johnathan scraped the soles of his shoes over the pebbles on the floor of the tunnel. 'Well . . . you needed some, didn't you? And I wanted it for myself, too.'

'But you knew it was unsafe . . .?'

'Well, I had intended to get the roof and top timbering off gradually—so that I could work peacefully on the bottom. Only there wasn't quite enough time.'

'You mean . . . because I said I must have the money for next Thursday?'

'Oh, I didn't think there was any real risk, Louise,' Johnathan said quickly. 'I reckoned if I was careful—and only came here alone—it would all last until I'd sifted through the rubble. That's why I didn't tell anyone what I was doing, or where I was working.'

'You told Beth . . .'

'Only enough in case anything happened; and she'd know to look in White's Gully. Not that I thought anything would!'

'You wouldn't have taken any risk at all, if I hadn't been impatient—made up my mind to go a week earlier, would you? I pushed you on, didn't I?'

'Oh . . . I don't know about that. Bruce was on my wheel, too—he and his mates. We're all after the same thing and our paths have crossed a few times. That's why they reckoned they had to discourage me. Didn't you, Bruce? Couldn't live and let live—too greedy!' Again the bitter rumble in Johnathan's voice. 'Anyway, you've certainly fixed this jaunt!'

'I hit him   that's why we fell in . . . and the roof,' Louise said, not because she was sorry for having hit Bruce but because she had to explain why the roof and the timbering had failed.

'If he hadn't fallen in he and his mates would have got in some other way,' said Johnathan bitterly.

There was silence then for a long time, so long that the blackness became almost as heavy as Louise's spirit. Despite what she had said about the roof failing because they had fallen on it, her only comforting thought regarding Johnathan was that she hadn't *known* he was going to risk his neck for her. And in regard to Bruce, she couldn't help wishing that

Johnathan didn't sound so bitter still, and angry. This darkness could become their tomb, and was not the place for anger. It was indecent, surely, to be angry about things that might never concern them again. Why, even now, God might be close.

And she said to Johnathan, 'What do you believe in?'

'What d'ye mean?'

'Well . . . like . . . after we die?'

Johnathan took a long time to answer, almost as though he resented her asking. He was the kind of boy who could go his own way alone, whose strength was his own strength; he didn't shun people—he hadn't turned away from Louise and her problem—but he had no need of the bolstering of others. Because of this his thoughts were his own thoughts, especially on such subjects as God. But he did answer at last.

'There's something . . .' he said; 'I'm sure of that. You've only got to look at a tree—it knows what it has to do . . . what it can do—and nobody tells it.'

'You believe in God?'

'Yeah . . . I reckon . . . something . . .'

'What is he like?'

'How should I know. I haven't seen him. But I know about a tree . . .'

She didn't ask Bruce what he believed in; she didn't want to embarrass him, in their present situation, seeing he pinched things. And she didn't ask herself—but she was comforted by Johnathan's 'something'. A tree was a good thing. The old apple tree, resting its trunk on bricks now, went on being what it was, every year, and nobody told it.

'Johnathan, you're really set on being an orchardist when you leave school?' This question seemed as silly as Johnathan's anger against Bruce seemed indecent, seeing that they mightn't be alive to leave school; but they had to talk about something, otherwise the blackness was more real than they were.

'Yeah. I want to work with trees.'

'But people say that the day of the land is over—that overseas markets are dwindling and that there is over-production here. They say that Australia's got too much wool, too much butter and cheese, and too many apples and pears.'

134

'I'm still going to grow apples,' said Johnathan. 'I like to see things I plant—or help grow—come to fruition. There's nothing more satisfying. And I reckon a bloke has to be what he has to be. You're trying to be just that . . . aren't you, Louise?'

But Louise didn't want the question tossed back at her, she didn't want Johnathan to examine her motives for what she did—only help her to do it. So she said again:

'People say that the rural industry is decaying—that the day of the small farmer is finished—that only the big companies will be able to make the land pay.'

'A big company, run from a city office, can't have any feeling for the land,' the boy said; 'a company wouldn't know what a tree really is—you have to get close to a tree. You've got to have a feel for it.'

And a ridiculous idea shot through Louise—what did she have a 'feel' for? Not a feel 'against'—like the red dress—but a feel 'for'?

Johnathan was still speaking. 'One thing's sure—people will always have to eat. So I'm going to grow apples. But first I want to go to Dookie.'

'Dookie!—the agricultural college—but it costs a lot of money to go there. And you have to have at least five Leaving subjects—including English and chemistry.'

'Yeah, I know. And it costs nearly six hundred bucks a year—for three years. I found out all about it.'

'Will your parents be able to afford . . .?'

'No, they won't be able to afford to send me there. There are three kids following after me. And I reckon the Supermarket'll get Dad and the Corner Store in the end. I'll have to help myself.'

'But how?'

'I'm saving up to buy a motor-mower, then I'll get week-end work cutting lawns in the town. While I'm at Dookie, I'll lump wheat at the wheat sidings over the summer holidays—that's good money. Or I'll go fruit-picking—a bloke can make a hundred and fifty a week if he's prepared to work fourteen hours a day seven days a week, and is a careful picker and doesn't spoil the buds for the next season. Both are outside jobs—that's what I like. Won't be any hardship.'

'Not many boys want to go on the land . . . now . . .' Louise said, putting him into a niche of his own, and followed up with: 'You've got a purpose, Johnathan—that's the same as having hope, isn't it?'

'I don't know,' Johnathan answered shortly. The niche made him uncomfortable and he found Louise embarrassing at times. He didn't want to analyse why he wanted to work with trees any more than Louise, a few moments ago, had not wanted to examine her motives.

'Your mother . . . she's practical, isn't she?' probed the girl.

'Yeah . . . but she's a good mum. I reckon she's sensible wanting me to go in for something that fits in with this computer age. It's me that's foolish. That's why I can't ask them to pay for it—something they don't believe in. But if I can get it for myself—that's different. These two bullet bottles could put me up twenty dollars.' Then he added hastily. 'But you can have the use of the money as long as you want, Louise.'

Bruce stirred on the other side of Louise. While Johnathan had been able to talk quietly about trees and his plans—as though even in this hole he was one with the earth—Bruce had had little to say but had been wriggly and restless in his cocoon of darkness. 'It's getting very stuffy,' he complained. 'Do you think it's getting stuffy—sort of airless?'

'What are you going to be, Bruce?' Louise asked. She didn't much care what Bruce was going to be, but they had to go on talking.

Bruce was as slow to answer as Johnathan had been, as though pondering something he had never considered before.

'I'll be an apprentice next year . . . to a builder,' he said at last, surprising himself at what he said, and the way he said it. He had grinned this morning when he'd heard his mother tell Eva that his father had gone to make arrangements to apprentice him to Mr Donovan, master-builder. But down here, in the dark, in the dark that seemed to be getting heavier and heavier—resting almost on the lungs—it seemed the most natural thing in the world to decide to be apprenticed to a

136

master-builder. Something solid and real, and very dependable —much more dependable than orchards were, where newer and stronger pests appeared every year, for which newer and stronger sprays had to be discovered. Bruce thought that Johnathan had stars in his eyes. But there were so many things a man could build, and work, with wood or like materials.

'My father was going this morning to arrange it with Donovan—his firm does most of the building and contracting for miles around.' Having said it, it was clinched, made very real, and Bruce settled back and, for a time, did not wriggle.

Louise drew breath deeply then, while she thought what a good idea this was for Bruce, but her mind was somewhat scatty now—jumping around a bit . . . from one thing to another, airy and light—and she thought again of Chan Ah-Foo, while every now and then she drew a deep sighing breath.

Maybe he had been friends with the Chinese publican and store-keeper, who had grown those peppercorn trees in the mullock heap, and which had hidden the cellar for so many years. Perhaps he had been in this cellar and in this tunnel. Not that the Chinese diggers went in for tunnelling a mine— 'stone-holing' they called a shaft with a tunnel. No, it was unlikely that Chan Ah-Foo had ever been in this tunnel. But he could have been in the cellar. She kept seeing his face— and now it was the face of the man they had seen in the cemetery, only he wore a pig-tail and a coolie hat, and shoes with wooden soles that turned up at the toes. She was thinking of Chan Ah-Foo's broken painting when Johnathan spoke.

'You haven't told us what you're going to be, Louise?'

'Me? I don't know yet except that it'll be something different from what I am. And away from the town. I'll have to live in the world. The world's a big place, you know. Some people never see it. Just being born doesn't make you alive.' Which neither boy understood.

Louise began to feel detached again as though she wasn't one of the three. Although it was dark she could see quite plainly all of them sitting there, sitting waiting. Bruce staring at his feet, irritated because they weren't carrying him out of this hole as they carried him out of most holes; Johnathan staring at the rock face opposite, having the patience to wait, like the waiting for the growing of a tree. And the girl—who was herself—both irritated and patient, but grateful for these pictures that her mind plucked, like sound waves, out of the darkness. It occurred to her that she should write down what she saw and felt—write down this experience. Though they might be going to die this was an experience of living.

'It's getting very stuffy,' said Bruce, and he coughed.

'Strike a match, Johnathan,' said Louise; 'we've been here a long time—and I can't hear anything yet. Strike a match. Give us a look at ourselves. So that we know we're not just turned into voices.'

Johnathan tried hard to strike a match. He struck three . . . four . . . five. . . . But while they flickered into life, they died instantly, as though an invisible hand snuffed out the flare.

'That's funny,' said Johnathan.

But they all knew what it meant. They were the youth of a gold-mining district, and even if there was scarcely any mining done today, they had listened through the years to stories of the mines. They knew that foul air—or gas—was extinguishing the match.

In the darkness, Louise felt Bruce quiver at her side, while Johnathan went taut.

'Gas is seeping in from somewhere,' Johnathan said stiffly; 'the fall of earth has moved something—shut us in—but opened a pocket of bad air.'

'How long . . . can we last . . .?' whispered Bruce.

'It's hard to say. The first matches I struck didn't go out— so the air was sweet then. But we don't know for how long, or how fast, the gas has been coming through.'

'When it will put a match out . . .' Louise began, very quietly, scarcely believing.

'I know, it's pretty thick,' Johnathan finished for her. 'There certainly won't be enough time now for anyone to find us and dig us out.'

'Carbon dioxide . . .' said Bruce, and his voice, somehow, was lazy and as unbelieving as the girl's.

'Stand up—get on your feet!' Johnathan suddenly ordered.

138

'I know we can't stand upright . . . but tł
air and is thickest at ground level. It pus
Stand up!'

There were awkward movements as tł
feet, but no quick stretching for the purer
tunnel, as though they were already apatł

They stood quietly, half-crouched or
height, no one willing, it seemed, to voice
had to not being dug out—in time.

It was Louise who deliberately shook heı
would wake it, and said: 'That leaves onl}
we'll have to try it.'

At once Bruce jerked as though a striı
from that simmer of laziness, and his arm
He gripped Louise's shoulder so hard that
banged her into the rock wall. 'Johnathan
remember! He found that it got almost
body . . . and that the roof would fall.
Johnathan. I'd rather the gas.'

Now it was Louise who caught hold of E
consciously forcing her feet to feel the rock
she seemed to be floating, and delibera
fuzzy mixed-up pictures of Chan Ah-Foo,
them waiting, from her mind. 'It *is* a chanc
there's *no* chance.'

'You go, I'll stay. Gas is painless—just goı
'*We're all going.* You have to make a bid t
there's a chance.'

'You will only get caught in there—jɛ
Jammed . . . think of it! And draught from that
let the gas reach you in time to make a quicł

'We have to try it.' Louise sounded quiı
quite calm, and her mind was very clear
this chance—their only chance—to get out o
start off. But I'll stop—and I won't move aı
you don't follow.'

She didn't know whether she meant what sł
she could stay back with this boy in the foul

still a thread of a chance to escape. But she did know that
o without him, to leave him to certain death, would haunt
forever if she herself escaped. And when Johnathan said
 won't move without you, Bruce,' she knew that Johnathan
the same.

he felt Bruce tremble, and realised the magnitude of the
ision they had forced upon him—the decision for their
ee lives—the terrible choice they were offering. It would
so much easier to yield to the gas—to drift into the blackness
the mind, as well as blackness of surroundings—to let go,
wait for it to happen—painlessly. In his body, close to her,
mbling, cold, she felt the battle that was in his mind.
She waited. She touched his hand again. 'Now,' she said.
e can't waste any more time.'
'You'd never give up, would you, Louise?' Bruce said very
ietly; 'you'd do what you felt you had to do.'
Louise could see nothing in the darkness but she felt she was
ring at the voice. 'I suppose so.'
'It would be so much easier if you would just go . . . and
ve me. I wouldn't mind . . . you leaving me,' Bruce said,
 voice tired.
Louise cried out then. 'I'm waiting on you! We're both
iting on you!' There was so little time.
Waiting on him! Waiting on him to decide between the
s—which was so much easier for him to face but which would
rtainly take his two companions with him—or the chance in
e tunnel, fraught with a possibility horrifying beyond con-
mplation. But nonetheless a chance which these other two
ere eager to take. With his face screwed wryly in the dark,
ruce knew he couldn't deny Louise and Johnathan this chance.
'Then . . . start . . .' he said.
Louise began to crawl forward, trying to make no noise so
at she could hear that Bruce was following. And presently
he heard him behind her . . . breathing in jerks . . . but
ollowing, and Johnathan behind him.
They crawled into thick darkness, but there were no more
matches struck. To see another match die would surely destroy
what was left of their morale.

140

CHAPTER SEVENTEEN

After finding the packed suitcase, Eva sat for a long time on the edge of Louise's bed. She was glad she was alone and able to cry freely, glad not to have to care whether her shoulders shook, or her stomach. Louise was going—really going.

In her hurt, she ran her fingers through her hair again and again, until it stood up in streaks of protest, and once she flung herself, full-length, on Louise's bed, and moaned.

Louise was the whole pivot around which she had built her life, working for her, feeding her, keeping this roof over her head. She had had no other real interest since the day Rosemary died. Somehow she had never been able to envisage the day when Louise would not need her, or this roof, when she would not be necessary to her. She had not been able to see any end to this maternal close relationship; or that one day Louise would be a woman herself. She had kept this house safe for Louise, and Louise for herself. Or—a thought that physically hurt—had she been hanging on to the house in case she was never loved . . . not even by Louise?

Eva felt that her whole life had been drained dry—that all that remained for her was the empty hulk of her body.

After pushing Rosemary's suitcase out of sight, she forced herself to finish making Louise's bed, to make her own bed, and to wash the dishes. Then she set out to walk to the bank chambers. She and Julia were both in trouble with their children; they could talk it over together. It was Saturday morning and the bank would be closed for business, but she hoped that Dan Burton would not be at home. He intimidated her. He had to do with so much money and could dictate even to the wealthy; he was a member of the Drama Group, president of the Historical Society, secretary of Rotary. He and Julia lived in a world that was so far removed from hers that it was too unreal even to think about.

But she and Julia had one thing in common, their children.

She went to the rear of the chambers, as was her wont, and Julia let her in. They sat down at the kitchen table, as they always did when Eva stopped for the morning-tea break, and now it was Julia who made the tea.

She said at once, 'Dan's gone out. He's gone to make arrangements for apprenticing Bruce to Donovan, the builder. He said Bruce can finish with ordinary schooling. He's not going to stand any more nonsense from him. He can be apprenticed . . . or make his own way. Dan's made up his mind.'

Julia spoke with a flat acceptance of her husband's edict; with the same flat acceptance that the local farmer or business-man showed when Dan Burton set a ceiling on their credit. 'It's a big change in Dan,' she said. 'He's never taken a stand like this with Bruce before—but I suppose Bruce had it coming. And I have to agree with Dan, I know he's right. But Eva—what's going to happen if Bruce says he won't be apprenticed to Mr Donovan?'

'To Donovan—here in this town?' Eva asked, drinking her tea in very small sips.

'Yes. Dan's term here has been extended for two years. He heard yesterday. A most unusual thing to happen—something to do with the depressed state of the rural industry and Dan being such a good consultant. We'll be here for another two years, at least.'

It was a relief for Eva to know this. Her job in this house, anyway, was safe.

They talked then, each telling her story of her child, interspersed with the story of the other child, and each ending up with a complete picture of the other's troubles. Eva even told Julia about the red dress.

142

'She's going soon," she finished, 'her case is packed. I don't know what to do.'

Julia smiled sadly. 'I didn't realise that she might feel this way about the dresses. But I should have known. She's very much an individual. Not that this is something about her that strikes you immediately—you have to get to know her—she's mostly a quiet person. Very quick and intelligent. She's doing much better than Sheila, although Sheila works so hard.' She looked at Eva almost appraisingly as though she wondered why this should be so.

Then she sighed over her own lack of perception. 'Yes, I see Louise's point, Eva—I wouldn't have worn those dresses, either. At least, not unless I was naked.'

'You wouldn't?' Eva looked at her, puzzled.

'No—not if I'd been Louise,' and left it to Eva to determine what she meant by that.

'I don't know what to do,' Eva repeated.

'You can't stop her,' Julia said; 'if you stopped her now, she would rebel in some other more violent form. But I can see a solution for you, Eva . . . go with her.'

'To town!'

'Yes. Don't look so shocked. It's a long time since you went to the city, isn't it?'

'Fifteen years.'

'I thought so. Not since the day Louise was born. Don't go for a holiday—I know you can't afford a holiday—unless you sell some of those antique pieces in your home. But go and work in the city with her over the Christmas period—you'll get a job behind a counter.'

'But I can't leave my jobs here—you and the doctor's wife.'

'I'll undertake to manage—and Rachel Henshaw can manage, too, for the time.'

Eva sat back, nibbling at the idea, but not biting into it. It was too big to bite at. In any case, she knew it was not the solution. Whatever was driving Louise to the city, away from her, was not going to be satisfied by her going along, too, for the ride, you might say. No, that was not the solution, with all due respect to Julia. She wanted to keep Louise at her side, but when Louise threw her off, she would never force herself on her.

They both sat quietly sipping, then Julia said. 'Your house is a collector's piece, Eva. I had no idea—until I saw it this morning . . . and the things in it. Those chests of drawers and your brass bedstead.'

'It's just old furniture,' Eva said: 'always been there.'

'Lots of city people are retiring up here now. It's no more than a pleasant country drive down to the city from here these days. An arty couple would rush your house. The whole thing is a collector's piece, Eva.'

Eva sat very still. The whole thing? She was part of it. She could see that Julia thought she was a collector's piece, too.

'I couldn't leave the house,' she said; 'and I need all my furniture. I couldn't buy more. You needn't tell Mrs Henshaw to manage . . . or yourself. I won't be going.'

And they were still again.

'Why don't you marry Arty?' Julia said, out of the blue.

'He never asked me again—after I said no—when I took Louise,' said Eva, and there was no telling whether she was disappointed or not about this.

'I still think your problem is easier to solve than mine,' said Julia, topping up her cup of tea this time, and coming back to Bruce. It had eased her tension for a moment to talk of Eva's antiques. 'Louise will probably marry, and someone else will have to worry about her. But a boy is different. The pattern he sets at this age usually sets the pattern of his life—Dan says so. A boy has to make his way in the world . . . all the time. He has to earn enough to keep a wife—a girl like Louise, or a girl like Diane, or a girl of some kind—and a family. But we don't seem able to get this idea across to Bruce. That's why Dan's finished with ordinary school for him—it's an apprenticeship . . . or nothing.'

Julia was sorrowful, and greatly disappointed in her son. A woman always hopes for something special from her son—seeing no limit to what a man might achieve, what leadership he might give. The fact that Bruce was handsome, and had potential, made her disappointment greater; because she knew he was never going to use it.

So the two women drank their tea and shared their problems and didn't hear Bruce get up from his bed; or know that he stood for a moment at the door, and grinned sourly at the talk of apprenticeship; or hear him go out by the front door that opened into the side garden. He just missed running into a Chinese gentleman who knocked on the bank-chamber's front door only a minute or two after he had closed it.

Julia opened the door to Mr Sung Chia, as his card identified him, and invited him in to the green lounge room with its two Chippendale chairs, eighteenth-century *cloisonné* vase and *Sèvres* shepherdess. Then when Mr Sung explained that Mr Burton had told him that the woman whose Chinese painting on glass had been stolen worked for Mrs Burton, and that he, Mr Sung, had come to find out more about the painting, Julia said that Eva must join them.

Eva would rather have gone home. She was not used to sitting in the green lounge room as a guest. The loss of the painting—the painting itself—was of no importance now. She felt that it was very unlikely that selling the painting would have kept Lou at home. Not when she was packed to go. That meant she was going.

But Eva was naturally polite, so she banked down her feelings about Louise and sat uncomfortably on the comfortable lounge chair and listened to Mr Sung Chia.

He was a very pleasant Chinese man, with smooth un-wrinkled olive skin, despite the years he claimed, and only a little grey in the neat, shining black hair. His eyes, too, were dark and shining.

He told them his grandfather had worked on the goldfields, that he had done very well and had sent home, in devious ways, many parcels of gold to his people in China. He had been a young man when he left Canton but he already had a wife and a family, and his own father, as the patriarchal head of the family, had cared for them, while the young wife had served parents, grandparents and children. The patriarch was a wise

145

man and used the money from the gold to build a fine tea-growing estate. The family had become rich—moving later into business in Hong Kong—and wrote constantly imploring the absent son to return home and share the happiness of the wealth his labours in *Hsin-chin-shan* had created. But the years went by and the consignments of gold—which the family no longer needed, anyway—became less and less, with long periods between. At last the absent one ceased even to write letters. They guessed what had happened to him; he had become a slave to opium—the cure and curse for loneliness and lack of his wife. It robbed him of the desire and will to go home. So he died in the land of 'New Golden Mountain.'

'Before leaving Canton, the grandfather had been an artisan painter,' said the Chinese visitor.

'And what was that?' queried Julia, while Eva wished she wouldn't ask questions because now that she had talked with Julia about her problem, she wanted to go home. She wanted to see whether the house was as desolate as she had left it this morning.

'It was the British who started it all towards the end of the seventeenth century,' said Mr Sung Chia. 'Through such chartered companies as the East India Company, they forced open China's commerce to the world, persuading the Chinese, with their unlimited cheap labour, to produce goods especially for export trade. Not goods that the Chinese particularly preferred or wanted themselves—but goods that the Company thought would sell well on the European market. In China, even today, a painting on glass is not rated very high in the world of art.'

'Oh . . . ' said Eva, thinking how foolish she was to feel sharp disappointment that her painting wasn't special. Yet surprised too that she could even feel. It made her realise how much she had relied on the painting being valuable.

'Many people were employed on these goods for export—all hand-labour, of course; it was before the time of the machine-made factory article. Whole concourses, or hongs, of people would be employed on doing one aspect of an article. My grandfather was very clever at painting on glass, but it was

146

still only a job . . . at almost slave wages. The hongs were along the Canton waterfront and it was here that he first heard about the gold-rush from the crews and touts of the East India Company merchantmen. And many other Chinese men heard about it, too.'

'Indeed,' said Eva, because Mr Sung Chia was looking directly at her. But she was thinking of the thief who had stolen the painting. *He* had considered it valuable enough to steal.

'My grandfather's family were very poor farmers then though he, himself, worked in a hong. They were always close to hunger. But they managed to save enough money to pay his fare to *Hsin-chin-shan*. He brought one of his paintings with him—not that it was his to bring, really, for his work belonged to his employer. But as he had no money after paying for his corner in the ship's hold, he thought it might help him in the new country—be a way of raising some money, if only a few shillings, in the new currency. As it turned out, he had no need to use it, for he was lucky with the gold, right from the beginning and kept the painting by him to remind him of his work in China. When I heard that such a painting had been stolen, I thought it might be the one.'

'There were many such paintings imported into the Colony and to the goldfields, Mr Sung,' Julia said; 'many Chinese merchants set up in Melbourne and imported all sorts of things from China—silks, tea, pottery-ware and such paintings. Not that there are many of them about now. It's easy to break a Chinese painting on glass.'

'This is true, Mrs Burton,' said the Chinese man. He turned to Eva, 'I read about your painting, Miss Turnbull. I would like to have seen it. Could you tell me more about it?'

'The main figures were women—seven of them—standing with their feet in the clouds,' said Eva mechanically, remembering Wang Lou.

'Heavenly Maidens,' nodded Sung Chia.

'And a half-circle thing—like a thin half-moon—across the sky.'

'The Celestial River: the River Across the Sky.'

147

'One of the seven was outside the circle—talking with another who looked like a man.'

'The Cowherd. The Seven Sisters and the Cowherd. It could have been painted by my grandfather,' sighed Sung Chia. 'I would have bought it from you, Miss Turnbull.'

'How much would you have paid me?' said Eva, alert for a moment to know the value of what she had lost, that is, if it had any value.

'Well, they're not worth a great deal. A well-preserved specimen might bring three hundred dollars,' said the Chinese man; 'I would have paid that for it whether it was painted by my grandfather or not. Just to have a relic of his gold days.'

Eva sighed, but had no words. She couldn't sell him the painting, anyway. It had been stolen.

Nor could she bear to listen further to what this Chinese man . had to say, though he was a very pleasant man with a smile that was like a light in his face. He said such a painting was not worth a great deal but to know that her painting may possibly have been worth three hundred dollars put an end to her politeness. She said goodbye to Mr Sung Chia and Julia, and went home.

CHAPTER EIGHTEEN

The house was very quiet and still, as though someone was dead, when Eva pushed open the back verandah fly-wire door, and then turned the key in the kitchen door which she always locked when she went out these days. But she was sorry she had forgotten to leave the fly-wire door propped open for Millie who liked to come and go at will on the back verandah. Millie was evidently huffed about the closed door, for she had not run to meet her as she always did, and this made the house seem even lonelier. Once she thought she heard the cat cry to be let in and went out quickly to look, but Millie was not there.

Eva made a cup of tea and ate a biscuit. Mrs Burton had extended the morning tea into a light lunch but she hadn't been able to eat much with Julia, not being used to having a meal with her employer. Then she started on her own house cleaning which she did usually on Saturday mornings. She didn't really want to clean the cottage now that it was afternoon, but she was too restless to sit, as she had done last week, and read the Saturday paper and make caramel toffee while Louise was away. Was that only a week ago?

Now and again she thought she heard Millie cry and each time she went quickly to the front or back door to listen, but the cry was never repeated while she waited. She worked at feverish speed, dusting and sweeping, and washing the kitchen floor, and taking no more notice of her furniture—collector's items, like herself—than she had yesterday. She worked so quickly that there was still some daylight when she finished.

She stood for a time then at the front door, looking across to the standing face of Ginger Gully where the ochre-tinted colours of the clay and gravel strata were made bold by the late time of day, and thinking of the young ones as they had left her this morning, not once looking back. Nor were they making any effort to return home early, she thought sadly. The last fifteen years of her life with Louise lay around her, broken in pieces, like this disturbed ground in front of her home. She began looking at each piece, from the very first moment when she had taken the baby into her arms—her young arms—and made it her responsibility to rear the child.

She stood there for a long time, noting that the rim of the gully was a sharp black line behind which a streaky gold-yellow sun was sinking into a bank of cloud leaving an immense stretch of fading blue sky above it.

Now she began to hear Millie crying again. A special kind of cry—a cry of pain yet not a cry of protest. This was the cry she had been hearing, off and on, while she was doing the housework. But why didn't Millie come to her?

Suddenly, she knew. Millie was having her kittens, some-where! Because the back fly-wire door had been closed she hadn't been able to get into the box, lined with clean paper and old rags that Eva had prepared days ago, and which Millie expected to be ready when her time came. Eva had always prepared her box for her.

Eva followed the sound now. Even in her own troubles, she had to find the cat and make her comfortable. Millie's cries—not very loud, but definite—led her to the side of the house and down the overgrown path. She soon realised that the cries were coming from beneath the house, close to the fuchsia bush and when she forced aside the scrawny, thick-stemmed bush she saw the bricks that Louise had placed there and the heaped-up rotted leaves and sticks. These were quite sufficient to block any view of what might be hidden under the house, but at one end was a space sufficient for a cat, even a fat cat like Millie, to squeeze through on her belly. It was dry and warm under the house, and it was natural that Millie should choose its shelter when her box on the verandah was closed against her.

Eva wondered about the bricks and heaped-up refuse as she

pushed and pulled them aside, but it was so long since she had seen behind the fuchsia that they didn't raise any real questions in her mind. She might have put them there, herself, years ago.

She called to the cat, 'Millie . . . Millie . . .'

And from underneath the cottage floor, Millie answered.

Eva had to break off some of the lower branches of the fuchsia so that she could get close to the opening in the wall, and then she lay flat and thrust in her arm to feel around for Millie, and called again, 'Millie . . .'

The cat answered, and Eva said again, 'Millie . . .'

Her right arm stretched far into the narrow space between the floor and the earth, sweeping in an arc. Her fiingers felt the square object wrapped in newspaper, thick newspaper, and then the cat on top of the newspaper, which no doubt was the nearest thing to her paper-lined box that Millie had been able to find. The cat answered with a satisfied whimper—the last of her three kittens had just been born.

Eva pressed her body closer to the wall of the house, scratching herself on the jagged ends of dead bits of fuchsia bush and slowly, with the one hand, she drew the oblong object wrapped in newspaper towards the opening. She moved it slowly, because Millie and her offspring made it heavier than it should have been.

When the first oblong end appeared, she knew at once what it was, and even the tiny wet kittens and Millie industriously beginning to clean them, couldn't absorb her attention, or account for the trembling of her body.

She eased the top layers of paper loose and carried Millie and kittens, as on a tray, to the back verandah and put them into the waiting box. She stayed barely long enough to note Millie's flexing of her claws in comfort as she settled into her rightful place, but hastened back for the picture. There on the path, crouching over it, she stripped off the rest of the paper, and saw that the painting was broken.

She didn't cry; she didn't even tremble now as she carried the picture back into the house, past the box and the cat, and laid it on the living-room table. She knew that only Louise could have taken the painting and broken it, and hidden it: and not admitted to doing so.

151

For a time she stared at the Seven Heavenly Maidens, and the Celestial River, and the Cowherd, and none of it made sense to her. Nor did Louise. Then she went to the front door again and looked once more over Ginger Gully. The sun was going down, and Louise would soon be home, and she didn't know yet what she was going to say to her. What were they going to say to each other when Louise came home? Suddenly, she couldn't stay still—by the door, or in the house, just waiting—but must walk and walk until she knew what she had to say. So she decided to go to a little farm on the outskirts, where they sold fresh eggs to people who cared to call for them.

But she didn't really need any eggs for she had got some yesterday, so she took a bowl to carry them but not any money to buy. She was not given to walking so the bowl was an excuse if she met anyone who asked why she was abroad— walking. She left the front and back doors unlocked as she went out, because there never had been a thief at all.

Scarcely fifty yards down the unmade track out on the road, she saw Mr Sung Chia coming towards her. He smiled widely and happily at her, his teeth so even and white for an old man.

'I am so glad to find you, Miss Turnbull,' he said; 'I want to hear more about your painting.'

She looked at him but she didn't stop, though she waved an arm towards the cottage. 'It's on the living-room table—take it—it's broke . . .''

'But Miss Turnbull . . . ?'

'It's broke . . . take it.'

She walked on thinking no more about him, only about Louise. She walked a long way; down the clay track, across the gravelled highway, and over the paddocks. She walked in the direction of the small farmhouse where they sold fresh eggs but she took a long, long way round.

The sky ahead was streaked with yellow on blue-grey; there was a faint blue evening mist over the paddocks and the hills and the trees, only the immediate grass was vividly green. Behind her in the west, low on the horizon, the bank of cloud was charcoal black now, and in the centre was the enormous red ball of sun. Red as Louise's dress. Red like danger.

And then she met Beth Baird.

The child started to cry at once, though Eva could see that she had already cried until her face was swollen and her eyes hidden in pink flesh. 'Miss Turnbull . . . Miss Turnbull!—they're buried in the cellar . . . the old pub cellar . . . in White's Gully!'

'Who? What are you saying?'

'Johnathan and Louise . . . buried in the cellar . . . in White's Gully! I went there after all—because Dora went home early—and I couldn't find them in the Gully but the three-legged dog was sitting there . . . and she was shivering . . . and she howled when she saw me.'

'What are you saying!' Eva was finding it hard to keep her hold on the bowl.

'They're buried under all the rubble. They're dead. They're dead!'

Eva grasped the girl then and shook her. 'What are you saying? What are you saying? Don't talk such nonsense!'

'It's not nonsense. They're in White's Gully—near where it forks. They're dead. I'm running home to tell my father.'

The child broke away, and left Eva standing there stricken, arms hanging, head bent. Then her whole body trembled and with great strides she went on to Slessor's farmhouse, the nearest. She was calling out before she reached the gate. 'Are you there, Bill Slessor? Are you home? Are you home?'

His young son came running, because the voice was so urgent. 'No, he went to the cricket and isn't back yet, Miss Turnbull. Mum says he'll be just having a Saturday drink,' said his son. 'Can I help you?'

'Give me a spade,' said Eva, and raced ahead of him to the toolshed and took a spade for herself. At the gate, she turned again, quiet now and practical as Louise could be, at times. 'Round up the men—all you can get from hereabouts. Johnathan and Louise are buried by a fall of earth—in an old cellar in White's Gully. Near where the Gully forks. Tell them to hurry!'

And she strode off, carrying her spade.

CHAPTER NINETEEN

If Louise and the two boys had had a torch, they could have moved fairly quickly along the main tunnel to the off-shoot that might lead them to safety. They would not have been able to walk erect, for it was not high enough even for Louise to stand upright, but they would not have had to go practically on all fours, feeling along the wall for the opening—the second opening—as they went.

Louise continued to lead, with Bruce directly behind her, and then Johnathan. Leadership had apportioned itself this time.

Louise had never thought of herself as a leader, and certainly had never been a leader among the girls at school; but when confronted with a choice that appeared, to her, to be no choice at all, then she was a leader. So she led forward, feeling a good deal of admiration for Bruce whose decision had been so difficult. And aware now that it was she, herself, who may have condemned all three of them to a slow cruel death.

Bruce kept very close behind her, bumping her now and again. Even while they were sitting in the thick darkness, he had touched her at intervals, as though re-assuring himself that she was still there. She wished he wouldn't. He was expecting more of her—a strength—that she might not possess. She dared not think how she might react if she did come to that point where there was not room enough to go on . . . if she were jammed. She only knew she had to go on as long as she could and that the boys would follow.

This second crawl along the black wet passage, however, was quicker than the first. It helped to have been through the tunnel before, to know that there were several deep holes that could be skirted only by pressing into the craggy wall, and that the second tunnel came rather quickly after that first dead-end. Behind them, urging them on, was the carbon dioxide.

Or was it with them all the way? Were they already breathing it in, poisoning their blood, filling their lungs, dulling their brain, with fumes they could neither see nor smell, until they slept and died, without knowing they did either.

Louise wouldn't let herself think of the gas, or whether her eyes were getting heavy and her limbs leaden. She crawled on, heartening herself with the thought that some fresh air must be coming in the hole through which they hoped to escape, and praying that Bruce and Johnathan would continue to follow.

They passed the first lead-off and came to the second.

'I'm turning . . .' Louise said over her shoulder to Bruce, 'after three or four more twists—four at the most—we should see the opening ahead.'

'D'ye think . . . it will be wide enough . . . for me to go through?' There was already the beginning of hysteria in Bruce's voice.

Louise was trying not to make her own fears real and was tempted to snap back, 'How should I know!' But she managed to say, 'I'll be ahead of you. I'll be able to tell you.'

She crawled on over ever increasing stretches of wet, feeling the mud beginning to cake on her and once a small frog leapt into her face. That was when her own hysteria·came close to matching Bruce's. She kept going only because she was certain that when they rounded the next bend the speck of distant light would welcome them and beckon them, and lead them. Light that was not only light but air—the clean free air of sunlight and warmth and blue of sky.

But when she turned the corner she cried out in disappointment and fear. 'It's gone! It's not there! The opening—it's not there!'

And from far behind Bruce—very far, it seemed, for there was not much space for even a voice to travel—Johnathan spoke for the first time since they had set out. 'That means its night. The sun's gone.'

For a moment Louise stopped crawling. Her disappointment hurt like a wound. During the hours she and Bruce and Johnathan had sat waiting in the darkness, she had been buoyed up by the thought of that eye of light. Not as an alternative way of escape, for the chance it offered was slight and fraught with such terrifying possibilities, but because it had helped her hold on to the fact that there was still an outside world, an outside world that filtered into this narrow, crouched cavern.

When they had started to crawl towards it, crawling away from the poisonous air behind, she had had an almost uncontrollable desire to get up and run towards it—to scream towards it. But her own practical sense—which was so completely the reverse, or perhaps the full cycle, of her imaginative side—had held her, soothed her, saved her, and in the blackness still led her.

Now it was not there. There was only blackness ahead; a blackness that grew narrower and narrower—she could feel it pushing on her shoulders, on the arms that elbowed her along, on her thighs where her jeans kept catching on sharp edges. Once the seam on a side pocket ripped and she was thankful for the layer of material that protected the flesh beneath it.

Now she stopped. The will to go forward left her. She smelled the smell of damp buried rock through which, no doubt, the fine lines of calcite were criss-crossed. A drop of moisture fell from the close ceiling on to the back of her neck which was stretched almost horizontal. She wondered if there were any other living thing in this tunnel except the frog. She remembered that most forms of life needed light. Near the entrance there might be some spiders perhaps, or even bats, but not here.

She was very cold, and Bruce's hand that reached out and touched her ankle was cold, too. Bruce had said nothing since he had asked his question in that high-pitched voice.

His touch moved her forward again. There was death behind but a faint hope of life ahead.

Although she couldn't see it happening, she knew almost at

once that the tunnel grew narrower. This narrowing was what had driven Johnathan back. She was able to crawl still but she was crouching more. In the heavy darkness she felt the walls moving in, beginning to clasp her. She wondered how soon they would begin to 'talk'. She began to crawl faster . . . faster . . . losing her caution for what she might meet. Somewhere ahead, even if she couldn't see it, there was that slit of light.

From behind her she heard Bruce's harsh breathing, and then a cry, 'Louise . . . Louise . . . where are you—I can't feel you. Louise!'

She didn't want him to touch her ankle. She didn't want to feel his trembling fingers.

'Louise . . . I . . . I want to push at this rock all around me . . . I want to push it out of the way. You do understand! My shoulders are . . . sort of . . . swelling into it.'

The roof . . . she thought . . . it'll fall!

'Keep crawling,' she said; 'catch up to me . . . I'm not far ahead.'

She stopped, hating to stop, and she felt his hand grasp her ankle. It was a tight, tight grip, a clamp around her foot; as she tried to press forward again, she felt his weight chaining her to him.

'Let go . . .,' she said, trying to keep her voice steady; 'you know I'm here . . . just ahead of you. Let go . . . I can't move if you don't let go.'

He let go suddenly, and she knew he was ashamed. 'I'm sorry.'

Funny, she thought, how darkness and nothingness all around could give you a glimpse of yourself.

The way became narrower. Louise was crawling flat now, elbowing her way along on her stomach . . . going forward into darkness, into she knew not what. Surely there must be some variation in the depth of dark ahead to show that there was an opening. It had been there earlier—that shining Oriental eye. Now there was nothing—surely there should have been a star. Was it possible that, somehow, they had taken the wrong turning, the wrong tunnel . . . that this didn't lead to that opening but just further into the middle of the earth? The track certainly seemed to be going down . . . going down . . . and she felt it should go up! This was indeed a freak tunnel, as Johnathan had suspected. Perhaps miners had cut the original, wider and higher, and had worked the gold through here, and then other miners had followed, yet never quite succeeding in closing this passage. This idea seemed to be borne out by the fact that every now and again she had to force her way over something that felt like a wooden beam or a bit of shaft timbering. Or maybe it was just one of these freak fissures or cracks in the earth's structure that had, somehow, connected up with the miners' tunnel. Whatever it was, it still led onward and still pressed in further and further until the rocks were wrapping around her. She realised then that, even if they wanted, it would be a physical impossibility to go back.

Louise knew that the boys must be in severe straits—that their wider shoulders, especially Bruce's, must now feel the actual clutch of the rock . . . that their elbows must find it hard to have freedom enough to propel them forward . . . that the weight of the earth must be resting on them. A weight that pressure, just light pressure, might start the rock 'talking'.

She heard the boys' grunts and uneven breathing; she heard the dislodgment of stones and she thought, in cold sequence, 'It's coming down. The roof's coming down. We're disturbing it—and it's going to fall. This is where we die.'

She struggled harder and faster, and wanted to scream when Bruce clutched her foot again.

'Keep going!' she called back, and it seemed that she shrieked. 'Keep going! Don't hold me—just let me go—and follow.'

If he hung on now, if he prevented her from going any further; if this sense of being jammed in on all sides finally took hold of him and he yielded to it—and hung on to her— then they were trapped just as surely as if the roof did fall in. Because Johnathan at the rear, working in such a confined space, would not be able to drag Bruce back, or break his hold on her. Without leverage even his tough muscles would be helpless. And, even if he could, to where would he draw back?

To the foul air in the wider tunnel? Preferable though to this kind of death. Bruce had been right.

'Let go, Bruce,' she said quietly.

'If it gets any narrower . . . I won't be able to get through— my shoulders are scraping!' he gasped. 'I thought . . . just now . . . I was wedged tight!'

She tried to turn his thought. 'How is Johnathan? Is he still coming?'

Johnathan answered. 'I'm right behind Bruce. My shoulders are scraping, too.'

It was a sombre voice and she realised that it was scarcely any easier for Johnathan than for Bruce except that he knew, if Bruce got through, there was room enough for him to follow.

'It can't be much further,' she said, 'we've been crawling for hours . . . it seems.'

'The wrong tunnel . . . perhaps . . . and no opening!' shuddered Bruce.

'No! No!' Johnathan roused himself to shout. 'No—this is the right tunnel—there was no other. Go on, Louise.'

It helped to have Johnathan give a directive like that; calm still, even if sombre, not giving up . . . helping her to do what she had to do.

Louise kicked her foot out of Bruce's grasp, risking striking his face and his cut lip, and elbowed her way on. She wormed through damp and cold and at times her long hair caught in a crevice or on some rough spike of overhead rock, as it did when she crawled under the apple-tree.

The apple tree . . . and Eva. The apple tree had been made safe to pursue its life and, although it was night, would be going on tirelessly with its task of forming its buds, and opening its leaves, and ripening its fruit. And Eva would be sitting in front of the living-room fire, reading the Saturday paper, and waiting for her to come home. She longed, suddenly, to hear the steady, colourless, dependable voice of Eva. And a red dress seemed a trivial thing.

Now there was a dreadful smell in the tunnel coming from somewhere ahead as though the earth was a creature with a bad breath; or else . . . or else some animal, a fox, perhaps, had crept into the tunnel to die, and she would have to pull herself over its decomposing body.

She was nearly sick. And then the thought leapt at her. If it *were* an animal—that must mean they were almost at the entrance. An animal—even coming in to die—would never retreat too far into darkness. They must be near the entrance— they *must* be near. The earth and rock pressed down closer, her arms and her elbows scarcely had room to move. The boys, with their wider shoulders, could they make it! 'Oh God', she prayed.

And then . . . the floor fell away from her probing, grasping hands, her shoulders eased out into a space that allowed their full expansion; her body wriggled and jostled forward, propelled now by her feet. She slipped into a kind of shallow basin and there straight in front of her was an oval slit of darkness that was grey compared to the inky blackness immediately behind her. The entrance! And big enough to allow them through.

But Bruce wasn't following! She felt around for the hole that had just disgorged her. 'Bruce . . . Bruce . . . come on! I've made it. I'm here—at the entrance.'

'You've made it!' There was surprise and disbelief in the words. 'You've made it!'

'Yes. Yes! Come on!'

Then he said, 'I'm stuck—I can't move an inch!'

Louise trembled to control her panic. 'Shrink . . . shrink your shoulders! Don't press into the walls—press into yourself. Shrink yourself. Bruce—I'm free!—d'ye hear? I'm free—you can be free, too!'

She leaned forward as far as she could into the narrow passage. 'Give me your hand—I'll try to pull. Push with your feet.'

She groped, but no hand came to meet hers. She screamed. 'Your hand, Bruce—give me your hand! It isn't just you—it's Johnathan—he's behind you. If you don't get out—he can't get out, either!'

'I can't! I can't move! I'm wedged in.'

'Johnathan! Johnathan!' the girl screamed. 'If you can

160

hear me—push him from your end. Start him forward. Johnathan—I'm out. Help him forward!'

Now a kind of moan came from Bruce as though he was someone coming out of an anaesthetic. 'You mean . . . you're out, Louise . . . you're free!'

'I'm free of the tunnel, Bruce . . . and I can see the outside night light. Try to reach my hand—try hard.'

She was partly back in the tunnel herself now, reaching in as far as she could, and Bruce's fingers found hers. They clung hard and Louise eased backwards. At first it seemed that the boy could not follow, that the walls were deliberately holding him. 'Shrink yourself!' she cried.

And somehow Bruce's bones stopped pushing against the rock walls, and yielded and contracted and dissolved into the flesh.

Louise pulled hard; Johnathan pushed as best he could from the rear and presently the boy's head and then his shoulders—those broad shoulders—emerged into the saucer of cave whose entrance was that oval of lighter dark.

Soon he was crouched beside Louise—still not able to stand upright in the shallow hole—and extending his arm towards Johnathan. Johnathan wasn't quite as broad as Bruce and followed slowly but surely into safety.

And when he, too, was crouched in the cave, Louise stepped towards the oval opening, knowing that she was stepping over the remains of the fox that she had smelled back in the tunnel, and feeling the webs of spiders that caught the insects that blundered through the entrance. It was not a big opening but by flattening herself she was able to thrust head and shoulders and arms through, and to feel with her hands whether there was any kind of ledge out on to which they could crawl. To her relief, she found that the ground seemed to slope gently downwards and that they need not fear crawling out into the nothingness of space.

Once out of the cave she stood upright, stretching her muddied limbs and feeling the joyousness of the free flow of her blood. The night was not moonlit but gay with stars and the wash of the Milky Way—the River of the Sky; a night that was

161

not all blackness but patterned with the light and shade of ochre-tinted earth and green bush and red rock, a night of sweet smells, even the burning of bush wood.

Across the gully with the ridges and hillocks that she knew were there even though she couldn't quite distinguish them because it was night, she saw the flares of burning torches and the light of fires. A century ago and more, a thousand camp-fires would have illuminated this spot like a myriad fireflies, but tonight the fires were grouped in a small huddle around what looked like a square. She knew at once that they were burning to light the way of the men digging in the cellar that had caved in.

'They're digging for us!' she cried and went forward on weak legs, trying to shout that they could stop digging now, that they were safe. But her voice was out of control, emerging only as a scratchy noise, as she swayed across the uneven mullocky ground.

Then she saw Eva. Eva using a shovel. Shovelling away with the score or so of men. Shovelling . . . shovelling . . . bending her back . . . straightening . . . lifting the great shovelful of gravel, throwing it aside, to take another from this fall of earth.

Louise stopped to gaze. There was scarcely any talking, not much noise at all, except the sputtering of the flare torches and the crackle of the fires, and the scraping of steel on gravel. She saw Eva's face. She saw the horror there, in strange new lines and crevices in her cheeks and dark circles swallowing sunken eyes, that had not been there when she left her in the morning. And the hopelessness of her shovelling was there, and sorrow. Only someone who loved could change in so short a time to look like that. In that split second—while she stood—looking at Eva's face, lit by the burning red of the fires, she saw Eva's love for her.

There were dozens of cars in the paddock that edged White's Gully, drawn up as close as they could be to the cave-in; there was Bairds' ute, the doctor's car, the police-car, the rescuers' cars, even the Burtons' car. For news had quickly spread through the town that there had been a cave-in and, with her own son missing, Julia had linked his disappearance with that of Louise and Johnathan.

And when the screaming laughter of relief and the weeping away of tension had ceased, and it was established that none of the three were actually hurt, rescuers wanted to carry them to the waiting cars, but they wouldn't have that, not even Louise. The cool sweet air had quickly steadied her weak knees, and it was good to feel the strength in her legs. Even the scratches and bruises sustained in the fall were forgotten. She could have skipped with Beth and Michael and Andrew over the dunes that the stars were lighting; indeed she could have danced to the Celestial River and the Seven Sisters and the Cowherd. But she wanted to shriek with laughter when she heard Michael grumble, 'We must've moved tons of earth—why couldn't they've walked out sooner—it was awful hard work.'

'Bet it was the bird's fault,' said Andrew.

But when Johnathan went off with his family, Beth hanging on one arm, and his mother on the other, she looked after him . . . surely, he would turn round or wave or something. Johnathan . . . Johnathan . . . her heart cried after him because she was fifteen, grown almost to a woman, and they had been through much together.

He did turn as he got into the ute, and call out, 'Hoo-roo . . .', but not specifically to her, but to Bruce, too, and everybody gathered about. How was she to know that now, when all the circumstances of this thing must out, that the responsibility for her fell from him like a fish shedding a hook. Johnathan was only fifteen, too.

She sat between Julia and Eva on the back seat of the Burtons' car and leaned towards Eva because she had seen Eva's face in the light of the fires—and something in that face that she knew would always be there no matter what she did or where she went.

She saw that Bruce sat erect on the front seat and answered his father's questions about what it had been like in the tunnel, how long they had been in there, and why they had gone there in the first place.

When they came to the cottage Eva invited the Burtons in,

163

but Julia said she thought it would be best for Bruce if he were to go straight home and have a shower to get rid of the mud, dry now, that was clinging to him.

Eva agreed. 'Lou'll want the same—and me, too,' she said. 'We get a good bath or a shower from the chip-heater—and Art filled up my chip-box only yesterday.'

'He does a lot for you, Eva.' said Julia.

'Yes, I suppose he does,' agreed Eva, as though she hadn't thought about it before. 'He dug very hard . . . in the cellar.'

'I heard Senior-Constable Hennessy ask if he'd like a lift home . . . he had the police car,' Julia said.

'I'm glad he got a lift,' Eva said simply; 'he worked hard.'

Then she got out of the car, and Louise followed.

'See you tomorrow,' said Bruce.

Louise followed her aunt into the living-room and when the lamp was lit there on the table lay the broken painting of the Seven Sisters and the Cowherd. There was a white envelope lying beside it, but it was the fact that her aunt knew now that the painting had not been stolen, but broken, that registered with Louise.

She stood quietly at the table, feeling drab and cold as she had in the tunnel, and when Eva picked up the white envelope, she noted her aunt's broken and torn fingernails, and the red welts and scratches on hands already toughened by work, and the clay dirt dried on her arms.

Eva took the note out of the envelope. She read it aloud, slowly, because she never was a quick reader and the writing seemed to have extra squiggles: 'I will give you a hundred and fifty dollars for the painting, Miss Turnbull,' wrote Mr Sung Chia. 'It is not a painting done by my grandfather but I would like to take it back to China—it is quite good of its kind. And the crack is in such a place that it can be re-fashioned into two pictures, a story told in two parts. I will call on you tomorrow.'

Louise and Eva stood for a long time looking at the painting. Louise would like to have said something about what she had done but, somehow, she felt that Eva didn't want it said.

'I think that Chan Ah-Foo would appreciate going back to China—his painting, anyway. Even in two parts,' she said at last. 'His bones, of course, can't go back. Who would know his bones from the other bones in the cemetery? They'll have to stay here always in *Hsin-chin-shan*, New Golden Mountain.'

'Yes, of course,' said Eva, and didn't say that she wasn't quite sure what Lou was talking about, except that she heard sympathy in the way she said it.

Louise moved almost reluctantly from the lamplit table: 'Now for that bath—it's going to be good—I'll wallow.'

'1 must stoke up the stove and get us something to eat—there are crumpets,' said Eva.

Louise went out on to the back verandah where Millie was purring over her kittens, to get the box of light kindling wood that Art had chopped.

'We'll eat the crumpets on the mat in front of the fire,' she called to her aunt; 'it was cold down there in that hole.'